Love
Undercover

Love
Undercover

JO EDWARDS

Simon Pulse
New York London Toronto Sydney

SIMON PULSE
An imprint of Simon & Schuster Children's Publishing Division
1230 Avenue of the Americas, New York, NY 10020
Copyright © 2006 by Johanna Edwards
All rights reserved, including the right of reproduction in whole or in part in any form.
SIMON PULSE and colophon are registered trademarks of Simon & Schuster, Inc.
Designed by Ann Zeak
The text of this book was set in Garamond 3.
Manufactured in the United States of America
First Simon Pulse edition December 2006
10 9 8 7 6 5
Library of Congress Control Number 2005937174
ISBN-13: 978-1-4169-2465-4
ISBN-10: 1-4169-2465-5

To my family

Thanks a million to my awesome agent,
Jenny Bent, and to my fabulously talented editor,
Michelle Nagler. You guys rock!

♥   ♥   ♥

A big shout-out to everyone who has supported me
along the way: Les Edwards, Paula Edwards,
Selena Edwards, Candy Justice, James Abbott,
Rachel Worthington, Chris Carwile, Hugo Reynolds,
Paul "Big Daddy" Turner, Helen Turner, Leslie Edwards,
Eva Edwards, Alan Turner, Sallie Turner, Leo Edwards,
Bert Edwards, Tommy Edwards, Laura Turner,
Waymon Turner, Debra Hall, Alicia Funkhouser,
Virginia Miller, Cheryl Hudson, Anastasia Nix, Velda Nix,
Teresa Johnson, Erin Hiller, Emily Trenholm,
Susanne Enos, William Clanton, Sharon Clanton,
Christie Griffin, Runi Afsharpour, Melissa Stroud,
Christy Paganoni, and Dr. James Patterson.
Thanks also to Wanda, Cheryl, and everyone at
Parkhurst Dental.

And last but not least, a huge thank you
to all my readers. You guys are what make
this whole thing worthwhile!

Prologue

I know what you're thinking. Sixteen-year-old girls can't be spies. But it happened to me. Yep, that's right. Most people find it hard to believe that plain, average, boring Kaitlyn Nichols would become a secret agent. But it's true.

Now, before you get too carried away, this isn't some crazy story like on *Alias*. I didn't single-handedly save the world from a nuclear disaster or apprehend a dangerous supervillain. Although, technically, I *did* help catch an evil hit man . . . but I'm getting ahead of myself.

I'm still new at this, so you'll have to cut me a little slack. You see, I never meant to become a spy—I kind of fell into it. Which is easy to do, since it runs in my family. My dad is an undercover agent for the FBI, which is totally not as glamorous and exciting as you might think. He spends most of his days completing paperwork, interviewing suspects, and analyzing case files.

But working for the FBI does have its moments. Every once in a while Dad gets to do something truly exciting, like rescuing a kidnapped woman or tackling a bank robber. And sometimes his work involves taking care of ridiculously hot seventeen-year-old boys, which is exactly what got me into this mess in the first place. . . .

One

Right this very minute, my mother is downstairs researching thong underwear. Or, more specifically, proper thong-wearing techniques. She's making all sorts of notes, like "for maximum sex appeal, let the top of the thong peek out above your skirt" and "guys find red thongs way sexier than black."

In a word: *ewww*.

Mothers aren't supposed to know about things like thong underwear. They're supposed to wear granny panties and leave it at that. But not my mom. Nope, my mom had to go and become the new sex columnist for the *St. Louis Observer*.

I know this is a big career break for her

and all. My mom's a journalist, and she's spent the past decade reporting on boring stuff like the shortage of garbage cans at Busch Memorial Stadium, or a city council member spending tax dollars to buy himself a new toupee. So I can kinda understand her wanting to branch out. But did she have to pick *this* particular branch? Couldn't she write about the latest Washington scandals or something? Instead, she's brushing up on all sorts of disturbing topics, like Miracle bras, condoms that are "ribbed for her pleasure," and—oh my God, I can't even believe I'm about to say this—vibrators.

It's a nightmare! Mom's new career venture is going to make me the laughing stock of Copperfield High—or *Cop-a-Feel* High, if you want to know what all the "cool" kids call it. Not that I'm one of the cool kids. Not by a long shot. Between my ridiculously skinny chicken legs, semifrizzy blond hair, pale skin, and so-flat-it's-practically-sunken chest, I'm not exactly the most stunning girl in school. And now Mom had to go and put the final nail in the coffin.

Thanks, Mom. I really appreciate it.

My best friend, Morgan Riddick, thinks I'm totally overreacting. "This is so not a big deal, Kaitlyn," she told me when I broke the news to her earlier today. We were sharing an enormous ranch chicken sandwich from Quiznos, which we do every Friday after school. It's sort of our start-the-weekend-off-right tradition. We go shopping at Union Station (which is this train station from the 1800s that's been converted into a shopping mall) and then we stop at the food court for an early dinner.

"It's not like this is the 1950s," she continued, taking a long, slow slurp from her Dr Pepper. "Everybody talks about sex these days. What do you care if your mom's writing a column on it?"

That's easy for Morgan to say. She and her mom have this total Lorelai/Rory Gilmore relationship going. They plan all these cozy girls' nights together where they sit around eating nachos and watching *The O.C.* As a matter of fact, when Morgan went to second base with Nathan Haverhill in the chemistry lab last fall, she actually told her mom about it before she called me! How abnormal is that? Naturally, I am thoroughly jealous. Morgan's family (which is basically just her and her mom) is amazingly cool.

Nothing like my whack-job parents.

I mean, seriously, my family is way weird. Not only is my mom a—*gulp*—sex columnist, but my dad's a secret agent for the FBI. Very few people know this, though. In fact, most of my friends think Dad sells car insurance. Technically, his undercover agent status can be revealed only on a "need-to-know basis." But, seeing how Morgan's my best friend, I figure she should be in the loop.

"You're so lucky," she always says. "Must be nice having James Bond for a father."

Sadly, my dad looks more like Dr. Phil than 007. And it's not like he's out there hunting down international villains or anything. He spends most of his days filling out paperwork and staking out suspected criminals' houses and stuff. It makes for long hours and, to hear Dad talk about it, it's excruciatingly dull.

"Like watching paint dry," he told me once. "You just sit and stare for hours on end and absolutely nothing happens."

Every now and then Dad will get called away "on duty." Usually, it's only for a week or two, but right now, he's been on some mysterious assignment for six weeks.

He never tells us much about where he's going or what he's doing. I do know (because I overheard Dad talking on his super-jumbo-encrypted cell phone one time) that he sometimes helps hide witnesses who are getting ready to testify. He doesn't have much to do with the actual Witness Protection Program (that's handled by the U.S. Marshals), but he helps protect witnesses at first before they get relocated. Dad catches them at that weird in-between stage when they're hiding out but haven't yet assumed a whole new identity.

I stand up from my bed and walk downstairs in search of Mom. I'm going over to Morgan's in a little while, and I want to know if I can take Mom's straightening iron. We're planning to give ourselves hair makeovers tonight and I want to be prepared.

Predictably, Mom's still hunched over the computer, hard at work on her thong investigation. "Kaitlyn," she mumbles when I enter the room. "You're just the person I wanted to see. Do you have a second?"

I shrug. "Morgan's mom is picking me up in half an hour," I say. "But I'm free until then."

"You're going to Morgan's tonight?" she asks absentmindedly.

I nod. "Yeah, don't you remember?" Mom's been a real space case for the past few days.

She pauses for a long time, and I halfway expect she'll tell me I can't go. "Ah, okay," she says finally. "I've been so preoccupied with this column and then with your dad being gone for so long, I guess I must have forgotten." She smiles. "Sit down, honey. There's something important I'd like to talk to you about."

Uh-oh. I decide to forget about the straightening iron and make a run for it as soon as possible. Mom has one of those my-baby-is-growing-up-so-fast looks on her face, which is never a good sign. And then I notice a book called *Teen Sex: The Shocking Statistics* sitting next to her computer. Which is pretty laughable. I mean, if Mom wants to have "the talk" with me, she's a little late. I'm sixteen, after all. I've known about sex since I was eleven. Reluctantly, I sink down onto the couch and brace myself for the worst.

"Let's just talk for a minute, you and me," she says, inching her chair closer.

"*Ohhh-kay*," I say, drawing it out. "What do you want to talk about?"

"Since I started working as a relationship columnist, my eyes have been opened to a variety of topics." *Relationship* columnist? Who is she kidding? The title of her column is *Sex Marks the Spot*. Pretty to the point, don't you think?

"Everything all right?" Mom asks, as I attempt to stifle a giggle.

"Sure, I'm fine," I tell her, putting on a serious expression. "Anyway, what were you saying?"

"Right," she continues. "Because of my new position as relationship columnist for the *Observer*, I've been given several topics to report on. The first, as you may know, is lingerie."

"Yeah," I say. "You're writing about thongs."

She blushes slightly. I still don't know how my mild-mannered mother is ever going to have the guts to do the job right. There's no way she'll be able to push the envelope very far. And thank God for that!

"That's true," she admits. "And to be honest, I'm a little put off by this particular topic. But next week's column is going to be much more interesting. Have I told you what it's about?"

Here it comes, I think, bracing for the worst. "No, Mom, I don't think you have."

"I'm writing about teenagers having sex," she blurts.

I think she expects me to be shocked, but I just shrug.

"Do you know enough about this topic, honey?" she asks, cocking an eyebrow at me.

I jump in surprise. I'm starting to panic a little bit. What if she's been listening in on my phone calls with Morgan? I mean, it's not like all we do is chat about sex, but the topic does come up from time to time.

"I'm not asking for personal experience, of course," Mom says. "But maybe your friends are having sex or are involved in, you know, heavy petting or other sexual activities. It's natural for teens to experiment, of course."

"*Heavy petting?*" I groan. I know what she's talking about, of course, but I've never heard it called that before. It sounds positively retro.

"Not that I'm talking about you *necessarily*, of course." She pauses. "But perhaps your friends are sexually active. Perhaps you have some, er, questions you'd like answered."

I am now thoroughly humiliated. Is she implying that *I* am having sex?

I am *so* not having sex.

"I want you to know you can always come to me, no matter what. And I would never use your name in my column, of course!"

"Of course," I mutter. I don't know what to make of this conversation—or my newly enlightened Mom. What kind of questions does she want me to ask? I may be a virgin, but I'm not *totally* inexperienced. I mean, hello! I did have a boyfriend for four-and-a-half months. (Although, for some bizarre reason, Mom and Dad seem to think my ex-boyfriend, Jared, is a total saint. I guess all his "yes, sirs" disguised the fact that he's a major horndog.)

"Look, Mom, I'd love to help you out here, but there's nothing I could add to your story. I'm just an innocent sixteen-year-old girl, remember? I mean, sex? What's *that* all about? I barely even know it exists."

I'm being a smart ass, but I don't really care. This whole conversation is totally patronizing. What does Mom expect me to do? Hand over a list with the names of the girls and guys in my class who are getting some? Tell her about my *own* experiences? As if.

She sighs her big, deep, you're-really-working-my-nerves-sigh. "Kaitlyn . . ." she begins.

I tap my watch. "Hey, I've gotta get ready to leave. Morgan'll be here in like fifteen minutes and I haven't even packed yet."

"Since when does it take you longer than five minutes to pack?" Mom asks. She breaks into a wide grin. "They could make a movie about you: *Packed in Sixty Seconds*."

"Uh, yeah," I say, cringing at her ridiculous joke. Can you see why this woman should not be writing a sex column? "Unfortunately, though, I look nothing like Angelina Jolie."

"Kaitlyn, how can you say that? You're very pretty!"

Oh no, she's starting in with the Mom compliments. "Well, I'd better go throw some junk in an overnight bag," I say, cutting the conversation short.

Mom looks like she's about to object when the phone rings. She glances at the caller ID, then begins shooing me out of the room. "It's Dad," she practically squeals. My dad has been gone on assignment for so long that it's become a big event whenever he is able to call.

"Can I talk to him?" I ask, hovering over her. Normally, I wouldn't be so eager, but it feels like Dad's been gone for a lifetime.

Mom ignores my plea and ushers me out of the room. I stop just on the other side of the door and attempt to eavesdrop. "Jim!" Mom says in an excited whisper as she answers the phone. I really have to strain to hear her end of the conversation. For some unknown reason, my mom always whispers whenever she talks to Dad on the phone. It's like she thinks the FBI has our line bugged or something.

"I miss you, too." There are a few minutes of silence, then I hear Mom go, "Kaitlyn's fine . . . tried to talk to her about this earlier . . . I know, Jim, but these kids today are sexually active at a really young age . . . No, of course I haven't talked to Dr. Gifford about it . . . Jim, don't start with me!"

I dart upstairs before I hear any more. Dr. Gifford is Mom's ob-gyn. The last thing

I want is for her to get any bright ideas about making me go in for my first gyno exam.

Back in my room, I begin shoving clothes and underwear into my overnight bag. I quickly finish packing and then head back downstairs to wait for Morgan. I'm surprised to find Mom crying softly in the living room. I knock on the door and then quietly let myself in.

"You okay, Mom?" I ask, perching on the edge of the couch. She's no longer on the phone with Dad, and her face is all tearstained and red. I hope they weren't fighting about me.

"I'm fine, honey. It's very tough with your dad being so far away." She smiles. "But I do have good news. He'll be coming home really soon—maybe even this weekend!"

I immediately brighten. "Really? Dad's coming home?"

"Well, it's difficult to explain," she begins, then stops. She looks like she wants to break something to me gently, but doesn't know how. She stands there stalling for a good minute, and then Morgan's mom pulls into the driveway and taps the car horn. "There's a slight complication."

"What kind of a complication?" I ask, ignoring the honk. And then, just to be cheeky, I break into the chorus of that Avril Lavigne song "Complicated."

Mom shakes her head. "You know what, don't worry about it. Really." She stands up and gives me a hug.

I'm totally baffled by her behavior. She's acting all menopausal or something. "But just a second ago you said—"

She shrugs it off. "Forget what I said. Just go out and have a good time with Morgan. We'll sort everything out tomorrow."

I start to ask her what she means by "sort everything out" when I feel her hand on my arm, pulling me up off the couch. A second later, she's opening the front door and waving at Mrs. Riddick.

"Look, Kaitlyn," Mom says, wrapping her arms around me for another hug. What is this, a Lifetime Television for Women movie? Why's she getting all touchy-feely? "What I was trying to say earlier is that I just want you to be prepared for change. I'm not one hundred percent sure about this, but I think our household may become a little more crowded. At first I was concerned, but I think you're mature enough to handle this."

Before I can respond, she gives me a firm push out the door. I stand there like a deer in the headlights, trying to absorb the weight of what she's saying. I feel pretty silly seeing as how I am literally trapped in the headlights of Mrs. Riddick's 2004 Saturn.

"Bye, honey," Mom says, slowly shutting the door in my face. I turn and hurry down the path. With shaky legs, I climb into the backseat of the Riddicks' car.

"Hey, Kaitlyn!" Mrs. Riddick says, smiling brightly. "How are you?"

"I'm fine," I say stiffly. Morgan swings around in the front seat and eyes me. She can tell something's up.

"What's going on?" she asks, raising an eyebrow. I put my finger to my lips, but she presses on. "Are you okay?"

I shake my head and motion for her to zip it. A terrible, awful suspicion is creeping its way into my mind. I try to push it out, but I can't.

"Seriously, you look ghostly pale!" Morgan continues.

Can she not take a hint? I rest my elbow

on the car window and then casually lean forward until my nose is peeking through the tiny crack between Morgan's seat and the door. "We'll talk about it later!" I hiss. The car lurches unexpectedly, and my head bangs hard against the back of Morgan's seat.

"Ouch!" I yell, rubbing my fingers against my sore noggin. It sucks that Morgan doesn't have her driver's license yet (she's not taking driver's ed until next semester) because then she could have picked me up alone. I have an intermediate license, which basically means I can drive wherever I want, just so long as I'm off the street by one a.m. (in Missouri you can't get a full license until you're eighteen). A lot of good it does me, since my mom never lets me take the car out without her or my dad.

"Kaitlyn, hon, put your seat belt on," Mrs. Riddick reminds me. "Safety first," she chirps ironically.

Numbly, I go through the motions, fastening my seatbelt into place. I don't want to say anything about my suspicions in front of Mrs. Riddick, though. I don't care how cool she is, she'd probably grab her cell phone and call my mom immediately. She'd say she wanted to "get to the root of the problem," when, really, it would be little more than nosiness. Deep down, parents are all alike.

Morgan keeps turning around and giving me funny looks. And I can barely keep still because I'm going crazy inside! This is just too strange for words.

The crying. The mood swings. The way Mom practically shoved me out of the room when Dad called so she could speak to him in private. Her words flash through my head. *No, of course, I haven't talked to Dr. Gifford about it. . . . Our household may become a little more crowded. . . .*

I take a deep breath and let it out slowly. There's only one thing this can mean.

My mother's pregnant!

TWO

"Of course I'll go out with you again," Morgan says, twirling the phone cord around her fingers. "Just so long as it's the two of us. I don't want you bringing your whole brood again, 'kay?"

I sigh loudly, trying to get her attention. We're sitting in the Riddicks' kitchen, and Morgan's been on the phone with her on-again off-again boyfriend, Nathan Haverhill, practically since we walked in the door. Apparently, Nathan's trying to convince Morgan to go see some new Keanu Reeves movie with him tomorrow night. Trouble is, last time they went out Nathan brought his little brother and sister along. "I wanted to get some face time with

Nathan, not babysit a bunch of rugrats," Morgan had complained afterward.

"Okay, sweetie, I'll see you around six then," she coos. After what seems like forever, she finally hangs up the phone. Her face is flushed bright red. "I can't wait to see him," she says, sighing. "It's been almost two weeks since we so much as kissed."

Involuntarily, I roll my eyes. The last guy I kissed was Jared, and that was practically two *months* ago. I don't feel her pain. "So, do you wanna hear my big news?" I ask.

Morgan grins and deadpans, "Big news? Me? Nah . . ."

I quickly fill her in on what happened before I left home. "So, as you can see, there's only one logical explanation."

"Hey, are you hungry?" Morgan asks, rummaging around in the cabinet for some food. "'Cause I'm absolutely starved."

"Morgan! Are you even listening to me?"

"Yeah, yeah, of course I am. You know what I think it is? Maybe your grandmother's coming to live with you for a little while," Morgan offers as she unfolds a bag of microwave popcorn.

I consider this. "No way. Gram lives in

this kick-ass retirement community down in Florida. She wouldn't give that up for anything."

Morgan places the bag in the microwave and hits pop. "Good point. Okay, then, maybe your dad's having an affair."

"Morgan!"

"No, no, hear me out," she says, holding up a hand to stop my protests. "Your dad's constantly going away on extended 'business trips.' You never know where he's going or when he'll be back. He doesn't even leave you guys a number to reach him or anything."

I roll my eyes. Now I'm wishing I hadn't told Morgan anything. "You know the deal with my father," I tell her. "He's an undercover agent; he has to go away on business."

"So he says. For all you know, he's banging some chick in Kansas City."

"My dad is *not* sleeping with some other woman," I say, purposely avoiding using the word "banging." Morgan can be so vulgar sometimes. "If he had a secret girlfriend, don't you think I'd know about it by now?"

Morgan shrugs. "Ignorance is bliss."

She has a small point, but there are way

too many flaws in her argument. If there's one thing my dad has taught me, it's how to analyze a situation. "Well, then, Ms. Smarty Pants, if my dad's having an affair, what does that have to do with our house becoming a little more crowded?"

"Hmm . . . that's easy. Maybe his mistress got kicked out of her apartment, so she's going to be staying with you guys for a little while."

"Yeah, sure. My mom's going to let some skanky 'other woman' move in with us."

Morgan takes the popcorn out of the microwave and begins pouring it into a bowl. "Maybe. Maybe not."

"Get off it, Morgan. My mom's preggers and you know it." I perch myself on a kitchen stool.

"Well, if you're so sure about it," Morgan says, "then just tell her you figured it out."

I make a face. "Puh-*lease*." I love her to death, but Morgan can be so dense sometimes. "Look, Mom probably wants to wait until Dad gets back in town so they can break it to me together."

"I still think you're overreacting," Morgan says, drumming her fingers against the countertop. "Hey!" she says suddenly. "Have I shown you Nathan's new profile picture?"

I shake my head.

"It's to die for! Come on!" Morgan starts toward the living room, motioning for me to follow her. She flips on her mom's laptop and pulls up MySpace.com. Both Morgan and I are huge MySpace fanatics. We spend hours every week updating our profiles, blogging, and posting comments on our friends' pages. It's one of our favorite pastimes.

Morgan logs on and finds Nathan's profile. At the very top is a cool-looking overexposed photo of him. His eyes are amazingly blue. Nathan's not my type, but I have to admit he looks pretty cute.

"Doesn't he look *hot*?" Morgan asks, pretending to swoon. "I mean, on a scale of one to ten, he's a twenty."

"He's pretty awesome."

"Just when I think I should break up with him, I think about those blue eyes and I lose all my nerve." Morgan sighs. "Speaking of hot guys, have you checked out the Copperfield section lately? Scott Ryder has a profile."

"Oh," I shrug, feigning disinterest. "Really. I hadn't noticed."

Morgan gives me a knowing look. It's common knowledge (well, common to Morgan and my other friends) that I have a ginormous crush on Scott Ryder. I've liked him since eighth grade. He's tall, with beautiful big brown eyes and sandy blonde hair. We sort of know each other—he works as the sports editor for the *Copperfield Courier*, and I'm the features editor, so we frequently run into each other in the newsroom and at staff meetings. Our conversations—all five of them—have been pretty limited, and I know it's pathetic, but I've memorized every detail.

The first time Scott talked to me was when he asked me to hand him a blank CD-ROM in the newsroom. The second time was when he asked me what time it was. Then he asked to borrow seventy-five cents and a pencil, respectively. And the fifth time—this is my absolute favorite—happened about a month ago. We'd just returned to school from Christmas break, and Scott and I bumped into each other outside the newsroom. One thing led to another, and we wound up in a fifteen-minute conversation.

It started when Scott asked me how my winter vacation was. I was nervous and caught off guard, so I rambled about how my dad made these excellent roasted chestnuts and the whole family enjoyed them. I mean, chestnuts! I even told him how much my grandmother liked them. Could I be any dorkier? Fortunately, Scott didn't laugh at me. In fact, he didn't say anything about the chestnuts at all. As soon as I'd finished talking, he launched into this long account of his family's eight-day tobogganing trip through Colorado. He told me about tobogganing down big hills, tobogganing down little hills, and tobogganing in deep snow and shallow snow. It was kind of a boring story, but I hung on to every word. I've never been so interested in tobogganing in my entire life.

Not that Scott would ever *date* a girl like me. He's movie-star hot and way out of my league.

Knowing all this, Morgan still has the nerve to ask, "So why don't you friend Scott?"

"No way," I tell her. "What if he denied my request? Can you *imagine*? I'd never be able to face him."

"He won't. He's got over two hundred and sixty friends. It's not like he's stingy about who he lets on his list. Come on, just go for it!" Morgan prods, pulling up Scott's profile. His gorgeous smile stares back at me.

I pause for a minute, thinking it over. "Nah, I can't do it. Besides, Scott has Amber Hamilton on his MySpace Top Eight. She's number *two*! The only person above her is his older brother, Timothy."

"That reminds me." Morgan groans, turning away from the computer. "Forget MySpace, and your mom's pregnancy scare. We've got *bigger* issues."

"Like what?" Secretly, I don't believe there *is* anything bigger than those two. Unless, of course, she's about to tell me that Chad Michael Murray asked her out.

"Amber Hamilton," Morgan says, spitting the name out like it's poison. "As in, how are we going to get revenge?"

Morgan's right. This *is* bigger.

Amber Hamilton is the reigning bitch of Cop-a-Feel High. She's so wrapped up in her own universe that she barely notices anyone else is alive. Or, if she does notice you, it's because she's looking for someone to torture.

Last week, Amber Hamilton declared war on Morgan. And by declaring war on Morgan, she also declared war on me. Here's what happened, in a nutshell: Both Morgan and Amber play on the girls' soccer team. On Monday they had team tryouts to determine who got which position for the upcoming season. Last year both Amber and Morgan were midfielders. But when a position opened up for a forward, naturally Amber wanted it. Even though she's not a very good player and can't run as fast as most of the other girls, she expected to land the coveted spot.

"It's because the forwards score all the goals," Morgan had explained. "Amber wanted to have the most high-profile place on the team." But then Coach Kleiger asked Morgan to try out and all hell broke loose. Amber couldn't handle the competition, so she did what any lowdown sneak does—she tainted Morgan's Gatorade with Ex-Lax. I'll spare you the heinous details, but let's just say that Morgan didn't exactly have a stellar tryout.

The irony is that putting Morgan out of commission really didn't do Amber much good—she didn't even make forward. A girl named Stacey Llewellyn did. God help her.

"She's a raging lunatic," Morgan fumes, shoving a handful of popcorn into her mouth. "I know how wrong it is to hate people, but when it comes to Amber, I can't help myself."

"It's unavoidable," I agree.

"You have no idea how much I despise her."

"I can kinda guess." I think about the Ex-Lax incident and shudder. "Just remember: Payback's a bitch. . . ."

The problem, though, was how to dethrone her. What could we possibly do that would ever faze Amber? It's not like she's threatened by our beauty. 'Cause, duh, Amber's a knockout. She resembles Mandy Moore, only with longer hair and bigger boobs. And it's not like we could throw our boyfriends in her face (not that *I* even have a boyfriend) because she's dated every fine guy at Cop-a-Feel. Well, all three of them. Of course, guys flock to Amber like bees to honey. In addition to being gorgeous, she's a megaflirt. She's always skanking around in these outfits that look like something Paris Hilton would wear.

"Maybe you could write a tell-all article,"

Morgan suggests. Her face brightens at the thought. "You could list her top ten worst qualities and stuff. Talk about all the guys she's hooked up with. We could launch a smear campaign in the school newspaper!"

"Uh, no," I say. "I could get in huge trouble." My job at the *Courier* is way too important to me to risk jeopardizing it with a stunt like that. Sure, the hours can be long, and we bitch about how stressful the deadlines can be, but secretly I love it. It's so much fun to interview people and write stories. I get to poke my nose into all sorts of situations I'd be shut out of otherwise. Besides, my big dream is to work for CNN as a special correspondent. After spending four years at Columbia University on a journalism scholarship, of course.

"Oh, come on!" Morgan urges. "What's she gonna do, sue you for slander?"

"Libel," I correct. "Libel's the printed word. Slander is when somebody *says* something bad about you."

Morgan snorts. "Maybe we should sue Amber for slander. God knows she's said enough bad things about us to last a lifetime."

"No lie."

"Have you ever stopped to think how pathetic our school is?" Morgan asks, shutting down the computer. "Why do girls like Amber get all the breaks when people like you and me get all the crap?"

"Yeah, we do get all the crap. Literally, for you," I say, grinning a little.

"Shut up!" Morgan says, but I can tell she's starting to chill out about the whole Ex-Lax incident. Which is a good thing. Right after it happened she couldn't stop crying.

We spend a half hour debating the Amber issue, but we're both stumped.

"Maybe we're thinking too high concept," I offer, laughing. "Instead of trying to come up with *one* huge plan, maybe we should launch a whole *series* of attacks. Like lots of little things that would add up over time."

Morgan shakes her head. "Uh-uh. We've gotta strike quick. And it's gotta be anonymous. If Amber knows it's us, she'll come after us big time. If we do, like, ten things to her, there's too much chance of getting caught."

"Yeah, maybe," I say. "But I still like the idea of hitting her with one thing after another. Kind of like a targeted assault."

Morgan cracks up. "Sorry there, FBI Lady. With all this talk of a 'targeted assault' and a 'series of attacks,' you sound just like your dad!"

I'm flattered. But at the mention of Dad, I'm instantly reminded of the whole soon-to-be-announced pregnancy. And suddenly I'm not laughing anymore.

"So did you bring the straightening iron?" Morgan asks as we settle down in her room to start our night of makeover magic.

"Nah. Mom's bizarro talk started before I could ask to borrow it."

"Hmm . . ." Morgan studies my face for a minute. "Maybe I can straighten your hair out with a blow dryer and a big brush. But first, we've gotta take care of your skin."

Self-consciously, my hands fly up to my face. "What's wrong with my skin?" I feel really lousy all of a sudden. I've actually been having a good skin day. Only two visible pimples, and they're both microscopic compared to the monster-size ones I occasionally get. But now, according to Morgan, my skin is a disaster.

"Oh, you're more or less zit-free," she

says. "It's your pores that are the problem." She reaches around and plucks a lighted magnifying mirror from her desk. The cord stretches just to where I'm sitting. "Here, take a look." She holds it up in front of me at close range. "You'd be amazed at the things you can see in this."

I stare at myself for a good solid minute. It's sobering. There's nothing more depressing than getting a microscopic view of your skin. Out of the blue, all these weird spots and holes and bumps and fuzzy places that have never, ever been visible before magically appear. And wrinkles! *Oh my God.* I actually have some little wrinkles around my eyes.

I MUST BE THE ONLY SIXTEEN-YEAR-OLD ON THE PLANET WHO HAS WRINKLES!

I start whimpering like some kind of a sick animal. "I have the most hideous face, Morgan," I wail.

Morgan quickly shuts off the lighted mirror. "It's scary, I know, but there's help." She jumps up and pads off down the hall into the bathroom. A few seconds later, she re-emerges, carrying a small green tube.

"Voila!" she proclaims, setting it down in front of me.

The label reads LOUISE BARTHOLOMEW-BRADDOCK'S PORE-MINIMIZING MIRACLE CREAM. "What the hell is this stuff?" I ask, screwing open the cap. It smells like a weak version of paint thinner mixed with stinky European cheeses. It's all I can do to keep from retching. The fact that the cream is this nasty puke green color isn't helping matters.

"It's a miracle cure, that's what," Morgan enthuses. "Seriously, put this stuff on every night before bed, and after two weeks your face will look brand-new."

"Oh, really?" I ask. I can't help being skeptical. I lower my nose and take another whiff, then immediately gag. "No way I'm wearing this junk. I'll vomit in my sleep and choke to death."

Morgan flips the mirror back on and lowers it to her face. "Look at this," she instructs. "Look at how even my skin tone is and how blemish-free I am."

I scoot over beside her and take a peek. "Oh my God!" I'm totally speechless. Morgan's skin looks *fantastic*. I mean, she could pose for the cover of *Teen People*, no airbrushing necessary. She's always been blessed with a virtually flawless complexion, but the magnifying mirror spares nothing.

"Unbelievable," I manage to whisper.

"I told you so. Don't knock it till you've tried it."

"Okay, okay, I'm sold." I dip my fingers into the container and scoop up a big glob of Louise Bartholomew-Braddock's Pore-Minimizing Miracle Cream and begin smearing it all over my face.

"Chill," Morgan cautions. "That stuff costs sixty-five dollars a pop."

"What!?" I yelp, dropping a big glob of green goo onto the floor.

"That's like five dollars' worth you just lost there."

I grimace. "I'll pay you back."

"Don't worry about it." She smiles. "It belongs to my mom anyway."

Now I feel worse. "Should we even be using this?"

"I use it all the time and she never notices," Morgan says. "I love raiding her beauty supplies. But if I had to choose, I think I'd rather raid your mom's closet. She has the cutest clothes."

Morgan's telling the truth. Even though I'm embarrassed that Mom's on the fast track to becoming some kind of a sex guru, she *is* actually pretty stylish. She's no Carrie

Bradshaw, but she's still very trendy. She buys all her clothes at Abercrombie and Banana Republic (last month, I even caught her scoping out a top at Wet Seal) and her shoulder-length blond hair is chopped into a really adorable bob. As much as I hate to admit it, she has a better sense of fashion than I do. It's not that I'm a disaster area or anything. It's just that I never seem to spend the time properly fixing myself up before going out. Every time I try to mix and match different outfits and jewelry and purses, I get totally overwhelmed and just throw on my favorite pair of jeans and a sweater.

I think I inherited my sense of fashion from my dad. And trust me, that's not a good thing. My dad is a major fashion victim. He goes around wearing these really ugly fuzzy sweaters every day. I think he owns about fifty of them, in a variety of Easter egg colors. As if that wasn't bad enough, he pairs them up with some yucky pastel plaid golfing pants. He's also got a passion for berets, because they mask his great big ol' bald Dr. Phil–looking head. It's embarrassing.

Case in point: Last month, my dad

showed up wearing one of his classic frou-frou outfits to Parent-Teacher Night. The next morning, I came into homeroom to find the words CAITLYN NICHOLS'S DAD IS A FLAMER scrawled across the chalkboard in big loopy letters. Which royally pissed me off for three reasons. First of all, it's not even true. Hey, just because my pop's favorite shade is light peach, that doesn't make him gay. And second, the person who wrote it (Amber Hamilton—who else?) didn't even have the decency to spell my first name correctly. It's Kaitlyn with a *K*, not a *C*. I mean, come on! If you're going to diss someone publicly, at least take the time to get her name right.

Last but not least, I was really bugged by how homophobic Amber is. There are several gay people at my school and I don't think it's cool to make fun of that kind of stuff. Even if my dad was gay, why would it matter? Who cares?

But that's Amber for you. Not a nice bone in her body. She's going to have a field day when she discovers that my mom has become a sex columnist. I can picture it perfectly. She'll laugh straight in my face, and then say something really sarcastic like

"Funny how your mom knows so much about sex when you're a hopeless virgin."

"So I think we should wait and style your hair tomorrow," Morgan suggests, staring at my head. "After you've washed it. As it is, you've got more pore-minimizing cream in your hair than on your face!"

I ignore her comment. I can't help it if I'm sloppy. Besides, I'm starting to feel downright prickly. "Hey Morgan," I say, as we get ready for bed. "This pore-minimizer stuff is really itching."

"Huh?" she asks distractedly.

I squirm around uncomfortably, trying to keep my hands off of my face, when what I really want to do is rake my fingernails over my skin to stop the itching.

"It itches!" I yelp. "My face feels like it's being eaten alive by mosquitoes!"

Morgan doesn't seem concerned. "Oh, it always does that. It itches for like twenty minutes, but then it stops." She flips off her bedroom light. "Just go to sleep. As soon as you drop off, you'll forget all about it. I promise."

Three

Famous last words.

"MORGAN!" I shriek, staring at my reflection in horror. "My face!" It feels like someone has dumped itching powder all over my skin. And I look even worse than that. Two words come to mind: chicken pox.

"What time is it?" Morgan mumbles, rolling over in her bed and pulling the blankets tighter.

"It's five a.m.," I tell her. "And I just woke up into hell."

"Oh, okay," she says, still half asleep. "That's cool."

This is so *not* cool. I'm two steps away from dunking my head into a bucket of ice. In fact, if I knew where the Riddicks keep their bucket—or if they even *have* one, for that matter—I'd go ahead and do it. I'm in that much pain.

"Help me," I plead. "You're the one who got me into this mess in the first place." Okay, so that's not entirely true. It isn't like she held a gun to my head and forced me to rub stinky European cheese–smelling goop on my face. But still. She's the one who *very strongly encouraged* me to do it. And that has to count for something.

"MORGAN!" I say again, louder this time. "I'm dying over here. Do you have some Benadryl or something?"

For some reason, this makes Morgan spring out of bed. "Benadryl?" she repeats. "Why?"

"BECAUSE MY FACE ITCHES LIKE MAD!"

She rubs the sleep out of her eyes and looks over at me. "Oh, crap!" she says, as the image registers. "What happened to you?"

"What happened to me?" I sputter. "Louise Bartholomew-Braddock's Pore-Minimizing Miracle Cream! *That's* what."

"You must be allergic," she says, shaking her head in surprise.

"Duh."

"Okay, hang on, I'll go track some down." She's gone for what feels like hours. In the meantime, I wash every last trace of the stuff off my face. Then I figure out a pretty clever way to scratch my face without risking major scarring. I begin rubbing my T-shirt against my face, trying to massage out some of the itch. When that proves too rough, I dig my satin bra out of my bag. It's smooth and cool to the touch, so that helps. There's just one problem. I'm a measly 32A, so there's not a whole heck of a lot of material to scratch with.

I sigh pitifully. This is just one more example of how being flat chested is destroying my life.

Thankfully, Morgan resurfaces with a pill and a bottle of calamine lotion. "What the heck are you doing?" she asks, catching me mid-scratch. She eyes my purple bra, which I'm holding up against my cheek.

"Don't ask," I say, and continue scratching.

"We don't have any Benadryl," she apologizes. "So I brought you one of Mom's Claritins."

I gratefully swallow it and then grab the calamine lotion.

"Now, I don't know much about that

stuff, but the label says it stops itching."

"I'll try anything," I say, pouring it into the palm of my hands. I rub it into my face and, thankfully, it's fairly soothing. It doesn't really take the itch away, but it deadens it.

"The price of beauty," Morgan says, giving me a lopsided grin. She crawls back into her bed and snuggles down to go to sleep. Within minutes, she's snoring. I'm still way uncomfortable, so I know there's zero chance of me drifting back off to sleep. I read magazines for a while, until it's not such an ungodly hour, and then I tiptoe in and beg Mrs. Riddick to drive me home.

"I'm sorry to wake you," I say, even though I can see she's already up and reading a paperback romance novel.

"Kaitlyn!" she exclaims when she sees me. "What happened to your face?"

"I don't know," I moan. I don't want to tell her I'm having an allergic reaction to her pore-minimizer. Then I'll have to admit I used it in the first place.

"It looks like you've broken out in hives," she says, her face marred with concern. "Get dressed and we'll go down to the twenty-four-hour Walgreens. Maybe the pharmacist can recommend something."

"No, that's okay," I tell her. "I just wanna go home."

"Are you sure?"

"Yeah." I nod. "We've got a bazillion ointments and creams in our medicine cabinet. I'm sure Mom can find something to help me out."

Mrs. Riddick doesn't seem convinced, but agrees to take me home anyway. We pull up in the driveway at a quarter past eight. I can't believe I'm fully awake so early on a Saturday. I thank Mrs. Riddick and climb out of the car.

"You sure you don't want me to come in with you?" she asks.

"No, no, I'm fine," I assure her. "Tell Morgan I'm sorry for bailing on her so early."

"Don't stress about it, Kaitlyn," she says. "Go inside and take a bath in baking soda. That'll help you feel better."

I'm not exactly sure a baking soda bath would do me any good, considering the problem is on my face, not my body. But I smile and thank her anyway. I'm just grateful to be home, where I can be miserable and hideous-looking in private.

I really do look awful. There's no getting

around it. Every inch of my face is covered in these enormous, gross red bumps. I look like I've broken out with a terrible case of measles! Making matters worse, my hair is a total disaster. Because I rolled over onto my side while I was asleep, the pore-minimizing cream got all over my hair. I'm in desperate need of a shower—and possibly a brown paper bag to shove over my head.

I fumble around with my keys and then let myself into the house. I can hear the sound of the TV blaring in the living room, so I drop my overnight bag and head toward the noise. Mom must be having trouble sleeping. Maybe it's a side effect of being pregnant. Don't pregnant women have to pee every five seconds? And throw up all the time? She's probably been living in the bathroom all night!

I sit down in front of the television. It's strange, because Mom left the channel on MTV, which she almost never watches. Obviously she's studying up on teenagers for her *Sex Marks the Spot* piece next week. They're playing a Black Eyed Peas video, so I crank up the volume and start humming along. As soon as Mom comes back, I'm going to confront her. I begin practicing my speech in a low voice. "I know about the pregnancy, and I'm okay with it," I say. "This is a big change for all of us, but I think I'm mature enough to handle it," I mumble to myself. "I'm ready, willing, and able to help out in whatever way necessary."

Wow! This is so good, I should be writing it down. After all, parents love stuff about maturity and responsibility. If I play my cards right, maybe I can swing a car out of the deal. Mom will probably want me to have reliable transportation. You know, because of the baby and all. Once she starts showing, she probably won't be able to maneuver a car very well.

I practice a few more lines. "I want to be there for you and Dad," I say. "I know how much stress you're under. I know that you need for me to—"

"Ahem."

I jump off the couch. What's Mom doing sneaking up on me like this?

"I know about the baby!" I blurt, whirling around.

"Excuse me?"

I'm face to face with a total stranger. Standing in front of me is one of the cutest guys I've seen in a long, long while. He's thin, with jet black hair and dark, piercing eyes. He kind of resembles Orlando Bloom.

"Hey, you're not Mom!" I exclaim.

He looks down at himself and smiles. "Nope, not the last time I checked."

I feel a major blush coming on. At least my allergic reaction is probably hiding it.

He takes a step closer. "They told me about you. Kaitlyn, right?"

How does he know my name? And who is this *they*? I slowly inch backward, putting some distance between us.

"This is kind of an odd way to meet, isn't it?" the guy continues. I notice for the first time that he's got a faint Southern drawl. That's not so unusual, considering Missouri borders Arkansas, Kentucky, and Tennessee.

"What are you doing in my house?" I ask, suddenly realizing the gravity of the situation. What if he's a burglar? *Oh my God.* It just figures. I come face to face with a fine guy and he's here to rob me! Then I think of Mom. A pregnant woman, and he's probably got her tied up down in the basement!

Unsure of what to do, I jump up onto the reclining chair. Thank God Mom left it locked in the upright position, or I'd have toppled right off of it and landed on my butt. I'm not sure why I got up here, but being taller than him makes me feel more powerful.

"Hey, are you okay?" the stranger asks. He's so soft-spoken that I can barely make out what he's saying. I hear something about "I'm sorry if . . . ," then his voice trails off. The next word out of his mouth is "blade."

HOLY SHIT! He's got a knife! He starts walking toward me, and I inch farther back on the chair. I wish more than anything that I hadn't dropped my overnight bag in the hall. I could have swung it around and used it as a makeshift weapon.

"Are you all right?" he asks.

"I'm f-fine," I stutter. My body tenses up as I try to recall any karate moves I might have seen. Should I leap off the chair and attempt to wrestle him to the ground? Should I make a run for it? Should I try to execute a quick one-two punch? Should I strike him first in the stomach, then in the head? My mind goes blank. I make a mental note to watch Jackie Chan movies more often.

Knife-guy continues to creep closer. Just

as I'm about to launch my attack, a familiar voice calls out. "Kaitlyn! What in the world's going on in here?"

I jump in surprise. "Dad!" I'm tremendously relieved. Everything will be all right now. Surely Dad can bust a move and take out the hottie intruder.

"I see you've met Blaine Donovan," he says.

"What?" I ask, startled.

Knife-guy waves. "I'm Blaine," he says and I realize, a few moments too late, that he'd been giving me his name, not saying he had a knife. I feel like a royal jerk. It's funny—the way he pronounces it, it sounds almost like *Buh-Laine*.

"Kaitlyn, I think we need to talk. Say hello and meet me upstairs, please," Dad says, gesturing for me to follow him.

I'm too stunned to move. Slowly, I climb down off my perch and onto the ground. Blaine's looking at me with a curious expression. The corners of his mouth are twitching like he wants to laugh but isn't sure whether it's polite.

"Nice to meet you," he says. He extends his hand. Reluctantly, I offer him my sweaty palm and we shake.

"I'm Kaitlyn Nichols," I mutter.

"I already know that, remember?" His eyes are positively twinkling now. "Why'd you jump up on that chair like that?" he asks, looking perplexed. "Practicing your best Tom Cruise impression?"

"I, uh, was, uh, feeling a bit panicked."

"It was kinda cute. Reminded me of those parts in the movies when someone jumps on a chair because they've just seen a mouse."

"Oh, uh, yeah," I mumble.

"Though I guess I'm a little bigger than your average rodent." He smiles.

I want to come up with some witty comment, something to make him think I have a funny, bright personality. But my mind goes utterly blank. All I can think about is that Blaine—this gorgeous Orlando of a guy—has called me *cute*. Me! Kaitlyn Nichols. It almost seems too good to be true.

Then I realize it is. After all, he didn't actually say *I* was cute. He said my *reaction* was cute. Big difference. My hand flies up to my face, and I feel like bursting into tears. For a moment, I'd forgotten how incredibly bad I look right now. I'm going on less than four hours of sleep and I look like I've broken out in a horrendous rash.

Duh! Of course Blaine wasn't flirting with me. He probably thinks I'm this big, pimple-faced, green-haired, sweaty-palmed freak. Just my luck that I look my absolute worst on the day the cutest guy I've ever seen appears right on my doorstep.

Four

You always hear people talk about how they were so embarrassed they wanted the ground to open up and swallow them whole. This is definitely one of those moments. Except being swallowed by the earth isn't good enough. I think I need to leave the planet altogether. Blast off in a rocket and take up residence on Mars or, at the very least, that weird space station thingy that's always on the news.

I attempt to smooth things over with Blaine. Because, when you're face to face with a gorgeous guy, what else are you supposed to do? "I'm sorry I got a little freaked," I say awkwardly. "I kind of thought you were a psycho killer and I was plotting my defense."

Blaine laughs. "Wow . . . I've been called lots of things before, but never a psycho killer. That's a new one. So what was this 'defense'? Were you gonna wrestle me to the ground? Pummel me with your brute force? 'Cause even though you're tiny, I bet you could do some damage if you wanted."

"Oh no! You're way too . . ." I almost say "hot," but catch myself just in time, "*nice* to hurt. Not that I wish harm on *un-nice* people. I mean, I don't wish harm on anybody. Not even Amber Hamilton, who is, seriously, my sworn mortal enemy." *Oh, God, why can I not just shut up?!* "It's just that I sometimes go a little ninja-warrior when I'm startled." It's true. I am very easily spooked. When Morgan threw me a surprise sweet sixteen party last fall, I got so startled when everyone jumped out that I stumbled and knocked over a potted plant.

It's so embarrassing standing here like this, talking to Blaine when my face is covered in nastiness. I mean, being around gorgeous guys is never easy, but this is worse than usual.

Blaine smiles and, for the first time, I notice how flawless his teeth are. Perfect and bright white, like he just stepped out of a

Crest commercial. "I'll have to remember that. Note to self: Never sneak up on Kaitlyn when she's watching TV if I don't want to get karate chopped. Since we're being honest here"—his eyes are twinkling like he finds this whole thing really amusing—"are there any other times when I should proceed with caution?"

Is he laughing at me or with me? Oh well, the only thing I can do is play along. Maybe he'll be impressed with my killer sense of humor. "Well," I begin, "when I'm cooking. Not that I'm much of a cook but, you know . . ."

"Right," Blaine says, pretending to make a list. "Lots of knives and forks and other sharp objects. I'll also steer clear of you when you're operating heavy machinery like cars or forklifts. Although you don't seem like the forklift kind of girl."

I giggle despite myself. "Forklifts aren't my thing. Tractors maybe."

"Okay, no messing with Kaitlyn when she's on a tractor." He laughs. "Any other potential ninja warrior situations?"

"When I'm listening to my iPod. Or showering. Definitely don't sneak up on me while I'm showering."

"You listen to your iPod while you're showering?"

"No, um, that's not what I meant. Oh, never mind."

Blaine blushes slightly, and I feel like an idiot. Why in the world did I bring up *showering* of all things? Now he's probably got this mental image of me naked. Not that I would *totally* mind him seeing me naked—if there were anything to see. I don't exactly have a smokin' hot bod like Amber Hamilton. When describing my shape, the word *twig* comes to mind.

Fortunately, Blaine changes the subject. "I've never been to St. Louis before. I don't have a clue what this place is like. You'll have to show me the ropes. You wouldn't mind that, would ya, Kaitlyn?" he asks, his Southern drawl kicking in.

"Sure, no problem. How long are you going to be in town?"

Before Blaine can answer, my dad comes thundering down the stairs. "Kaitlyn, hon, I really need to talk you," he demands, sounding very stern and fatherly. "What's taking you so long?" Dad's usually pretty cool and laid-back, so I don't understand his strict tone.

"All right, all right, I'm coming." First Dad brings over this weird visitor, then he freaks out when I play nicey-nice with the guy. This is all very strange. Usually Dad's thrilled when I make small talk with his guests.

I grab my overnight bag out of the hall and cut through the living room to the staircase.

"Let me get that for you," Blaine says, appearing at my side. He really does have a nice accent. I still can't place it.

"Oh, it's no problem. This thing only weighs like five pounds," I say, slinging the bag over my shoulder to show how light it is. Apparently, I don't know my own strength because I sling it much harder than I intend to. The back of the bag slams into Mom's bookshelf and sends a bunch of stuff flying. And I do mean *a bunch*. Mom is the world's biggest pack rat. I always tease her that she's going to become like those hoarders they show on *Oprah* if she doesn't start picking up after herself.

Blaine begins gathering up the mess, sorting through papers and stacks of books and setting them back on the shelf. "The two of us are gonna tear down this house if we aren't careful."

Despite my mortification, I giggle. I mean, really, you just have to laugh at yourself in these situations. I think I've set a record for hpm—humiliations per minute. Maybe that means it will be smooth sailing for a while. After all, I've racked up enough embarrassments to last me the rest of the year.

Suddenly, I spy a flash of material among Mom's papers. Wait a minute. Isn't that . . . sheer leopard print? And then I see another piece of material. Bright pink, this time.

Oh God, no. This is not happening. The stack of thongs for my mom's article—most of them still in the packages, thank God—are splayed out across the floor!

"I'll get those," I say, reaching down and scooping them up. It's too late, though.

He's seen them.

Blaine gives me a slightly bemused look. "Man, that's some collection."

"They're not mine," I quickly say. "They're my mom's."

"Uh-huh," Blaine says, smiling. He picks up the rest of the papers, then turns and walks away.

"Kaitlyn!" Dad says when I reach the

top of the stairs. "Looks like you've finally finished your ten-minute hike upstairs. Next time, try not to get stalled for so long at base camp."

"Whoa, easy on the sarcasm," I mutter under my breath. But to Dad I simply say, "Sorry, I was chatting with Blaine."

Dad's tone softens, and he places a hand on my shoulder. "Oh, good. I'm glad you two were getting along. I appreciate you making Blaine feel welcome."

"Well, the way you were yelling for me to get upstairs I never would have guessed," I say, before I can stop myself.

Dad smoothes his thinning hair down against his scalp. "I was worried you might be calling Morgan or one of your other friends to tell them about Blaine. I had to get to you before you did that."

Whoa. Why doesn't he want me to tell anyone about Blaine? After all, it's not every day I come home to find an adorably cute guy in the middle of my living room. It's a juicy piece of news, and I definitely want to share it with my best buds. "What's up with the cloak and dagger routine?" I ask. Even though my father is an undercover government agent he rarely acts like one. He's usually the most low-key guy on the planet. My mom is way more mysterious than him most of the time.

"I didn't want you to put anyone in danger," Dad continues.

In danger? Is he joking? "Are you feeling all right, Dad?" I ask, playfully putting a hand on his shiny bald forehead. "'Cause you're acting way weird."

Dad motions for me to keep my voice down. "Your mother's still sleeping. You don't want to wake her."

Oh, right. The pregnancy. Between my mega facial eruption and the Blaine surprise, I'd totally forgotten. I give Dad a sympathetic glance and nod knowingly. "Mom probably needs all the sleep she can get right now, things being what they are . . ." I say, letting my voice trail off.

Dad gives me a strange look. "She had a late night, if that's what you mean. We all did. Blaine and I didn't roll into St. Louis until almost two in the morning. And then we stopped at IHOP for a quick bite before coming to the house. Your mom was still up working on her column when we got here."

"You and Blaine sound awfully chummy," I say, eyeing him. "Scarfing down French toast in the middle of the night like old pals."

"Something like that," Dad says, and then motions for us to go in my room. "It's best if we have some privacy. This is a very delicate situation."

"A delicate situation?" I repeat, pushing open the door to my bedroom.

Dad follows me inside and takes a seat in my desk chair. "Let me give you the particulars."

I hate when Dad says things like that. It's usually a lead-in to some kind of lecture. Like the particulars of my grounding, or the particulars of my driving privileges. Whenever he uses the word "particulars," it means I'm about to get shafted.

Dad looks me square in the eyes and says, "Blaine's going to be staying at our house for an undetermined amount of time."

I raise my eyebrows in surprise. "What do you mean Blaine's going to be staying here?" I ask. "You're kidding, right?"

He shakes his head.

"And what do you mean by an 'undetermined amount of time'?" I ask.

"Blaine may be living here for the next

couple of months. Possibly until the end of the school year."

My jaw drops. I was expecting him to say *days*, not months. "What do you mean Blaine's going to be staying with us for a couple of months or longer?!" I exclaim, not that I'm totally opposed to this idea. "What is he, some long-lost cousin I've never met?"

Dad chuckles. "Funny you should say that. In a way, yes."

A sick feeling comes over me. Oh my God, *I've been flirting with my cousin!* Ick! I'm as bad as some of those jacked-up people Mom writes about in her column. "Which side of the family is he on?" I ask, thinking, *I've been to tons of family reunions, both on Dad's side and Mom's—and I have definitely* not *met Blaine before.*

"My side," Dad says. "At least, that's what his paperwork will say."

"His paperwork?" I dump the contents of my overnight bag on the bed and begin sorting through the mess.

"Yeah, his new driver's license and school records. The central office should have them ready in a day or two."

I'm totally lost. None of this is making

sense. "Why does Blaine need a new driver's license? Did he lose his or something?"

Dad shakes his head. "No, but it's standard fare for situations like this. It's all part of Blaine's FBI cover."

Suddenly, I get it. Everything Dad's been saying clicks into place. "Oh my God." I can't think of anything else to say. So I just stare at him, shocked.

"As you know, part of my job at the FBI involves keeping tabs on witnesses before they go to trial," Dad continues. "Usually we store them at a safe house or in a hotel for a couple of weeks before they testify. Basically, we do this to keep them out of harm's way so the bad guys can't get to them."

I nod. "Right. I understand."

He takes a deep breath. "Kaitlyn, what I'm about to tell you is classified information. You can't breathe a word to anybody. Not even Morgan. Can I trust you?"

I've never seen Dad like this before. He looks deadly serious. "Of course," I tell him. And I mean it. I'm great at keeping secrets. Whether it's something major, like Dad's profession, or some insignificant, gossipy secret, I always keep my lips sealed. Like the time I found out our friend Aimee's little brother was sending Morgan secret-admirer e-mails. Morgan thought the poor spelling and grammar were because they were from this cute French exchange student named Luc. Since he'd already gone back to Paris when I found out, I figured there was no harm in hiding it. What Morgan didn't know couldn't hurt her, right? It's good for her ego to believe a French hottie was into her.

My dad stands up and starts pacing the room, swinging his arms back and forth as he walks. As he gets to the far wall, his left foot bumps against my mile-high stack of magazines, sending back issues of *Teen Vogue*, *Cosmo Girl*, and *Seventeen* toppling over with a crash. Dad keeps right on walking. He doesn't even notice the magazine meltdown, which is weird since, unlike Mom, he's a major neat freak. "Have you ever heard of Harlan Donovan, the Texas oil tycoon?"

I shake my head. "No, but I'm guessing since his last name is Donovan he's related to Blaine."

Dad stops pacing, thank God, because his right elbow is about an inch away from my DVD collection. "Good guess. Harlan is Blaine's father."

"And I'm also guessing that if he's an oil tycoon he's probably a . . ." I pause, gulping, "millionaire."

"Add a few zeroes," Dad says, "and you're about right."

"He's a billionaire?!"

"Yes, he is."

"The real deal?" I ask, astonished.

"The real deal."

For some reason, this strikes me as funny. "Millionaires," I muse, "are so passé." It's true. Nowadays everyone—from Paris Hilton to Mary-Kate Olsen—is a billionaire. And they exclusively date other billionaires, too. I just read an article about it in *Us Weekly*.

Dad looks confused, but he doesn't stop to ask. He just continues with the story. "One of the business deals Harlan Donovan is involved in has been attracting a lot of attention lately. The wrong kind of attention. I can't go into the details, but threats have been made against Harlan and his family—and many of these threats have been targeted at Blaine specifically. We're currently investigating the situation, and we think the people involved may be responsible for strong-arming several other big oil deals. We're trying our hardest to catch them, but at this point in time, we felt it was best to remove Blaine and place him in a safe house until all of this can be resolved. Once we catch these thugs, or once the business deal is finished—whichever comes first—Blaine will be out of danger, and he can return to the Donovan Estate."

The Donovan *Estate*? "So why is Blaine staying here? Since when does *our house* qualify as a safe house? You've never brought any of the people you're protecting here before."

"The Blaine situation is complicated," Dad says, "and I can't give you all the specifics yet. For now, what I need you to do is not mention Blaine to anyone. *Not a word.*"

I nod my head. "Don't worry. You can count on me. There's just one thing I'm worried about. Won't keeping him a secret be kind of tough? Three months is a long time. What if Morgan drops by unexpectedly and sees Blaine? What if she calls and he answers the phone?"

"You won't have to keep him a secret for

that long," Dad explains. "Only the next couple of days. Once Blaine's new ID and paperwork come in, we'll be able to get to work establishing his cover. I'm not one hundred percent sure, but I think he's going to be posing as a distant cousin. That's what I meant earlier when I said that in a way, Blaine was a member of the family."

I chew on my lower lip. I'm feeling nervous about this, like I won't be able to do it. "So I'm going to have to pretend Blaine is related to me?"

Dad massages his temple, like he's got a headache coming on. "Something like that. I'll give you the full details as soon as I have them. I can't really tell you much more at the moment. What I need now is a guarantee that you'll keep this on the down low."

I giggle at his lame attempt to sound cool. "Sure, fine," I say, waving my hand dismissively. "I'll do whatever you need me to."

"Great! We can talk about this more later," Dad says, standing up and heading for the door.

"Okay." Without meaning to, I reach up and start picking at my cheek. The calamine lotion must be wearing off, because all of a sudden my skin's itching like mad again.

"Hey, why is your skin so red?" Dad asks, noticing my face for the first time. For an FBI agent, he's not very observant.

"It's from this pore-minimizing cream Morgan had," I admit, ducking my head in shame. "I'm going to kill her for getting me to try this."

Dad studies my face for a minute. "Is it supposed to make your skin that color? Because that seems a little counterproductive. What's the use of 'minimizing your pores' if you're going to turn blood red and swell up like a blowfish?"

"Allergic reaction," I tell him. "It's not a big deal." It's funny how just a few minutes ago, my skin seemed so important. But now, after hearing about Blaine's ordeal, it seems absolutely trivial.

"Allergic reaction, eh?" Dad struts over and ruffles my hair. "Well, it's not too bad. I'm sure it will clear up in a day or two." He gives me one of those I'm-really-counting-on-you-to-do-a-good-job looks as he says, "I really appreciate your help with the Blaine situation. And remember, not a peep." He makes a little chirping noise like a bird. My father is such a cornball sometimes.

"Point taken." I try to digest everything

Dad has told me. It's pretty freaking unbelievable. Dad's never been the type to bring his work home with him. Although, in this case, I don't really mind. A cute boy is welcome in our home any time as far as I'm concerned. "So what's Blaine going to do while he's here?" I ask, as Dad makes his way to the door. "I mean, won't he be bored out of his mind just sitting around the house all day?"

"Oh, I thought you realized. That's part of why Blaine is staying here," Dad says, giving me a *duh* expression. "The spring term just started at his old school in Texas and it'd be a shame for him to get too far behind in his studies. At first we were planning to get him a private tutor, but things worked out for him to enroll at Copperfield. So, starting in a couple of days, he'll be going to school with you."

Oh, boy. Blaine Donovan at my high school? This is going to be . . . interesting, for lack of a better word. I know Amber Hamilton, for one, will be thrilled. She always makes it a point to cozy up to hot guys. She's going to freak when she sees Blaine.

"I trust you'll show Blaine around and

make him feel at home? Going to a new school is stressful for anyone, and Blaine has been through a lot lately."

"Of course I will," I tell Dad. And I mean it. I'm going to do whatever I can to make Blaine feel welcome.

"And another thing," Dad says, looking me dead in the eyes. "I don't want to alarm you, but it would probably be a good idea to keep your eyes peeled for anything suspicious while Blaine's in town. Not that we expect anything will happen. We've covered his tracks pretty well, but you can never be completely sure. In some ways, Blaine's life is in your hands."

I feel all the color drain from my swollen face as this sinks in. *His life?* Good grief, I can barely take care of my *own* life. Just last month I sprained my ankle while trying to rearrange my closet (I was pulling a box down from the top shelf when I slipped and fell). How am I supposed to protect this hottie?

I must look pretty panicked, because Dad immediately adds, "That probably didn't come out right. What I meant was, I'd like for you to keep an eye on Blaine, just make sure nobody treats him oddly or takes an unnatural interest in him."

"What do you mean by 'unnatural interest'? Be real, Dad. Given Blaine's looks, I'm betting lots of girls at Copperfield are going to take an interest in him." I feel kind of silly saying this. It's not often that my dad and I chat about cute guys.

Dad gives me a half smirk. "That kind of thing would be considered a *natural* interest. I'm talking about if someone is overly friendly to Blaine, or starts asking a lot of strange questions about him. Most of this is guesswork. You'll have to rely on your gut instinct. Again, I don't expect anything to happen, but if you notice anybody behaving strangely toward Blaine, let me know ASAP. Got it?"

I scratch one of the spots on my face. "Got it."

"Also, be careful of any strange phone calls. Like if someone hangs up when you answer. Or if we start getting a high volume of calls that show up as 'unknown number' on the caller ID display. I've instructed Blaine not to answer the phone while he's here. I think that's safest. And if anybody calls here asking for him, you let me know *immediately*. If that happens, we've got an emergency situation on our hands."

"Wow," I say, twirling a strand of hair around my finger. "This is totally bizarre." I feel like I've been dropped into somebody else's life.

"I have confidence in you, Kaitlyn. You can handle it." Dad smiles reassuringly as he walks out the door. "Just think of yourself as a junior undercover agent."

At those words, a chill runs down my spine. *An undercover agent.* A spy. I feel electrified, energized. Almost like a mini Sydney Bristow. Except with shorter legs. And frizzier hair.

Five

You can't be a good spy without proper training. I have heard my dad say this a million times. But where to start? It's not like I can just sign up for a class. Last time I checked there weren't any spy schools listed in the Yellow Pages.

The obvious choice is to ask my father, but I really don't want to. The last time I got Dad to teach me something—driving—it turned into a huge disaster. He was a real drill sergeant. Every time I made any small slipup, like signaling too late or breaking too soon, he went ballistic on me. Things went from bad to worse when he decided to put a Styrofoam cup filled with water on the dashboard to teach me about being a cautious driver. If I made any sudden moves or went over any bumps too fast, the water would spill all over the place. I tried to be careful, but then this little frog hopped out in front of the car and I had to slam on the breaks to avoid hitting it. Next thing I knew Dad was drenched and, thus, our driving lessons were over.

No, I can't ask Dad for help. I know spying is his specialty, but I'll just have to be resourceful and find another way. Resourcefulness, I'm sure, is an important trait of top undercover agents. You probably have to know how to make a parachute out of a paper clip, or something equally complex.

I take out my algebra notebook and begin jotting down ideas:

1. Internet resources
2. Spy books (check school library)
3. Netflix *The Bourne Identity* and James Bond films
4. Borrow *Alias* DVDs from Morgan

I stop when I get to four. That seems like a good start. Plus, I can't think of anything else. I boot up my computer and type "spy tips" into the search engine. The first couple of sites aren't very useful—mostly things about "corporate espionage" and how to keep people from hacking into your computer. No James Bond–like tools. I change my query a couple of times. Finally, after some careful searching, I stumble on a website containing *The Ultimate Spy Manual*. Now we're talking! Unfortunately, *The Ultimate Spy Manual* costs $39.95 to download. My mood falls. There's no way I can pay that. I don't have a credit card—my parents won't let me—and Mom would definitely notice if I charged it to her account. I have to settle for the free five-page preview.

Luckily, the free preview turns out to be awesome. Lots of valuable information. I hit control and *p*, and as soon as the pages spool out of the printer I sit down to study them. The very first paragraph warns about the dangers of cell phones, cordless phones, and baby monitors. Apparently burglars and spies alike can use them to eavesdrop on you and obtain all sorts of classified intel.

We don't have a baby monitor, thank God. (Although I guess that will all change soon.) But I've got to do something about our other security breaches. I stare down at my desk where my cordless and cell are both sitting out in plain view. Who knew they were so dangerous?

I rummage around in my closet until I locate my old Winnie the Pooh phone. It's a huge plastic clunker, and I haven't used it in nearly ten years, but it will have to do. I unplug my cordless and hook up Winnie. I feel safer already. Sure, it looks a bit silly for a sixteen-year-old to have a Winnie the Pooh phone, but that can't be helped.

Now, what to do with the cell phone? I debate taking the battery out and locking it in my desk for safekeeping. But then what would I do if there was a real emergency? Like if Blaine and I were out shopping one day and some savvy bad guy came after us. Wouldn't it be better to have a cell phone than not? A spy could waste precious minutes trying to find a working pay phone. After much internal debate, I decide to hang on to my cell. The risk is worth it. I'll just try not to talk on it when I don't have to.

Next, *The Ultimate Spy Manual* talks about checking for bugs and wiretaps. I'm all engrossed until I get to the part where it mentions how expensive it is to perform a "sweep" of a property. It talks about how you need hundreds of thousands of dollars worth of high-tech equipment to even get started. Geez. So much for bug-proofing our house.

The next section of the manual is more helpful. It gives a list of important tips to keep in mind:

> *Be suspicious of strange deliveries, unexpected knocks on the door, and strange cars or vans parked outside. When driving, take unusual routes and switch lanes often to avoid being followed. Check mail for signs of tampering. Always ask for ID of anyone who tries to enter your house—from cops to TV repairmen. Be careful when throwing away any valuable personal information. Spies frequently rifle through garbage in search of clues.*

I read this over several times, trying to commit it to memory. Once I've got a good handle on it, I pick up the phone and dial Morgan's house. I think I've done enough spy research for today. I could use a break. Plus, I need to ask to borrow her *Alias* DVDs.

It takes forever for Morgan to answer the phone, and I nearly hang up. Finally, on the fifth ring, she picks up.

"*Mmm-hello*?" Her voice sounds muffled.

"Morgan!" I cry, louder than I mean to. "What are you doing?"

"Sleeping." She clears her throat. "What time is it?"

"Almost eleven o'clock."

I hear her fumbling around, probably getting out of bed. "I feel really bad about your rash. Is it any better? 'Cause it looked awful when you were here."

"Oh, yeah, it's better now. Hopefully it will fade before school on Monday," I tell her. "But enough about that. I've got something to ask you. Do you still have the *Alias* DVDs?"

"Every single season." Suddenly she sounds wide awake. "Even season five, which was kinda crappy with what they did to Michael Vartan's character and all."

Morgan is in love with Michael Vartan, along with about ten other TV actors. I honestly don't get it. She has an actual boyfriend who really likes her. Why does she waste her time daydreaming about fantasy men? "Well, can I borrow the DVDs?"

"No prob. You're gonna fall in love with the show, I just know it!" She pauses, thinking it over. "But what's with the sudden interest in *Alias*? You've never liked it before now. Every time I tried to make you watch it, you threw a big fit. You always said it reminded you of your dad and all his spy junk, thank you very much."

Uh-oh! Morgan's right, I *did* say it reminded me of Dad. I've got to come up with a cover. "Well, I . . . I sort of had a change of heart. It was one of those, how do I put it . . ."

"Cut to the chase, Nichols."

Lately Morgan has picked up this habit of calling me by my last name, as if she's Summer on *The O.C.* At first it was kind of cute, but it's starting to get annoying. "I'm trying to, Riddick," I reply snarkily. "I just keep hearing how it was a great show and all. So I thought I should try it out. Just because it's about spies doesn't mean I have to associate it with my dad."

As if on cue, my father's voice comes booming down the hall, floating through the walls of my room. "Don't worry, Blaine, our Kaitlyn's going to help you out every step of the way. As soon as we get your new ID—"

Oh, crap! Dad's rambling on at such high volume Morgan's bound to overhear him! In an attempt to cover the noise, I start talking as loudly as I can. "SO WHAT ARE WE GOING TO DO TO AMBER?" I shout. "HAVE YOU THOUGHT UP ANY GOOD REVENGE PLANS YET?"

"WHY ARE YOU SCREAMING?" Morgan asks, matching my tone.

"I'M NOT SCREAMING, THIS IS MY NORMAL VOICE!"

"NO, IT'S NOT!"

"YES, IT IS!"

"Kaitlyn, you're acting like a psycho!"

I try to come up with a clever retort, but my mind goes blank.

"Hey, what's all that noise?" Morgan asks suddenly. "I hear a bunch of guys talking. It sounds like they're right in your room."

She *has* heard Blaine and Dad blabbering on about fake IDs! Why does my father have to talk so *loud*? Didn't the FBI teach him anything about being secretive? "It's the TV," I lie. "I'm watching a *Laguna Beach* marathon and I've got the volume cranked way up."

She doesn't buy it. "Are you *on* something, Nichols? There's no *Laguna Beach* marathon today! MTV's playing back-to-back episodes of *The Real World* from morning till night."

I can't believe I'm so dumb. Morgan's a total TV-aholic, so of course she knows what's airing. She practically has *TV Guide* committed to memory. I think fast. "Right, well it's not on *now*. But I TiVo'd the *Laguna Beach* marathon last time MTV aired it and I'm just now getting around to watching it."

She pauses. For a tense moment I worry that I've been caught. But then Morgan laughs and says, "You're so weird, Nichols. Who waits a month to sit down and watch five hours of *Laguna Beach*?"

I barely see Blaine for the rest of the day. He spends most of the time resting in the guest bedroom, watching TV, and playing on the computer. I try not to take it personally. Maybe he's just tired? Maybe he's having trouble adjusting? Or maybe he's miserable being here—my parents certainly take some getting used to. But I'm sure Blaine is too polite to say anything.

But as the weekend goes on, something else occurs to me. What if the reason he's been avoiding the family is because he wants nothing to do with us? What if he thinks we're not good enough for him? After all, Blaine's so good-looking and rich. He's nice enough when you first meet him, but deep down inside he's probably a giant snob. Guys like that are always stuck up, right? It's just one of those sad-but-true facts of life.

But it's my duty to protect him, and I'm going to take that seriously. I read over the spy manual so many times I can practically recite it in my sleep. They ought to test us on this kind of thing in school. Seriously. Learning about secret agents is way more interesting than trigonometry and world history. And probably a whole lot more useful, too.

Six

Morgan grabs me the second I get to school on Monday. "Why didn't you tell me!" she hisses in my ear. "I thought we were best friends! You're supposed to fill me in on stuff like this."

I swallow hard. Oh my God, she knows about Blaine! She didn't buy my *Laguna Beach* lie after all. How am I going to weasel out of *this* jam? "Well, I . . ." I scramble, trying to think of something to say.

"Not here," Morgan says. We're standing in the front entrance hall, which is packed with other students. She grabs me by the elbow and starts pulling me up the stairs.

"Hey," I yelp, "my homeroom is back that

way." I've got exactly six minutes to get to my desk or I'll risk a tardy slip. My homeroom teacher, Mr. Clemmons, is a major stickler for tardiness. He'll write you up if your butt's not firmly planted in your seat when the eight-thirty bell sounds. Last week he gave me a late slip for being mid-sit when the final bell rang. Seriously, my butt was like five inches from the chair when he got me. No matter how much I argued it, the jerk wouldn't budge. And two tardies in a month gets you a week's worth of detention. I eye my watch nervously. Whatever Morgan has planned, it had better be quick.

Morgan leads me down the hall and into the chemistry lab. "Look," she shouts, whirling around dramatically and pointing to the blackboard. There, written in big, fancy lettering with blue chalk are the words MORGAN RIDDICK HAS GEEK STINK BREATH!

"Can you believe this? Isn't it harsh?" Morgan demands, looking like she's about to cry.

Ouch. That *is* harsh. And it's not even true. I stand there for a minute, surveying the damage, and then say, "This is so Amber Hamilton."

"Well, duh!" Morgan puts her hands on her hips. "Of course it's Amber. She's all about zinging people on chalkboards. Remember what she wrote about your dad that time he wore the pink outfit? What did she call him, a flamer?"

"Yeah," I grumble, "thanks for reminding me, Morgan."

"Sorry." She looks so bummed out. "Hey, your skin has almost cleared up."

It's true. I'm amazingly lucky. By last night the blotchy rash had faded to just a few pale pink spots on my cheeks and forehead. I covered them up with some concealer this morning and was good to go.

"Why didn't you tell me I have geek stink breath?" Morgan asks, remembering her own predicament. She covers her mouth self-consciously. "And what's up with that phrase? I've heard of nasty breath, but geek stink breath? That's so strange."

"It's the name of a Green Day song from like ten years ago," I tell her. "Scott Ryder has it on his iPod. He's podded up practically every Green Day song ever written, come to think of it."

Morgan puts an arm on my shoulder. "Oh no, Nichols, you've got it bad."

My face flames up. "I do not."

"You do so. How did you get a hold of Scott's iPod anyway?" Morgan asks, leaning against a lab table and fiddling with a plastic test tube. "Did he lend it to you or something?"

I laugh. "Yeah, *right*. What universe are you living in? He walked out of algebra class last month and left it on his desk. I merely picked it up and returned it to him. And, you know, I just happened to scroll through his playlist while I was at it."

Morgan giggles. Then her hand flies up to her mouth again. "I still can't believe you didn't tell me about my rank breath. You're my best friend! You're supposed to tell me junk like this, even if it hurts my feelings."

"There's nothing to tell you!" I insist. "Your breath is *fine*. Someone's just being an ass."

"You promise I don't have geek stink breath?" Her lower lip is trembling. "You promise you're telling me the truth?"

"Of course!"

She doesn't seem convinced. "I've never, ever had bad breath before? *Never ever?*"

I give it to her straight. "Well, your breath's not mountain spring fresh when

83

you first wake up in the morning, but that's completely normal. Nobody has good breath prebrush."

"I guess so." She still looks upset. "Why would Amber write that if it's not true?"

I sigh. "Because that's what makes Amber *Amber*. She's a mean, nasty beeyotch. It's not enough that she's fantastically popular and dates tons of guys. She's not happy unless she tears everybody else down."

Morgan slumps against the lab table. "Thank God I found this before classes started. I would have died if anybody else had seen it." She picks up a chalk eraser and wipes the board clean. "I ought to write something nasty about Amber in retaliation," she says. Then she snaps her fingers. "Yeah! That's a great idea." She grabs a piece of chalk. "What should I write? How about 'Amber Hamilton has hair extensions'? No, wait, what about 'Amber Hamilton is a two-faced liar'? Is that mean enough?"

"Come on." I take Morgan by the arm and steer her out of the chem lab. "We've got barely thirty seconds to get to homeroom," I say, glancing at my watch. "We can figure out how to get back at Amber later."

Morgan seems depressed, but she agrees.

"How did you find that anyway?" I ask, as we scurry down the hallway and toward the stairs. "What were you doing in the lab this early in the morning?"

She bites her lower lip, all embarrassed-like. "Nathan and I sometimes go up there to make out before homeroom."

"You never told me that!" I exclaim.

"I know. I'm sorry. It's kind of our little secret." She gives me an apologetic look. "You're not mad, are you?"

"No way." We jog down the stairs side by side. "I know we're best friends and we tell each other everything. But, you know, I think it's okay to keep tiny little secrets." Tiny little secrets like Blaine Donovan.

She seems relieved. "Cool. Thanks for understanding, Nichols."

When we reach the first floor, Morgan turns right while I dash left toward Mr. Clemmons's homeroom. I've just rounded the corner when the late bell rings. "Noooooo!" I wail, unable to stop myself. I'm not even close. There's no way he'll give it to me. Clemmons is a total stickler for punctuality. I debate skipping homeroom and hiding out in the bathroom until the first period bell. But Mr. Clemmons is also my English teacher. If I ditch homeroom and then show up for fifth-period lit class, he'll write me up. I have no choice. I have to face the music.

I creep through the door to homeroom, trying to look inconspicuous. No dice. Mr. Clemmons looks up from his attendance ledger and fixes me with a steely glare. Even through his glasses, his beady eyes look menacing. "Well, well, well, Ms. Nichols. We were about to send out the search and rescue squad for you." He takes out a piece of paper and begins writing.

"I'm so sorry I'm late," I tell him, struggling to catch my breath. "I had an emergency," I lie.

"Ms. Nichols, I am not interested in excuses, unless they come with a note from a parent," Mr. Clemmons says, pushing his glasses farther up his nose. "Do you have documentation from either one of your parents?" The corners of his mouth turn up into a small smile.

"No, but—"

"Then this matter's settled." Mr. Clemmons stands up and hands me a late slip. "Looks like they'll be seeing you in detention starting this afternoon."

Seven

"I forgot to give this to you earlier," Morgan says as I sit down across from her at the lunch table. We usually eat with a group of girls from Morgan's soccer team, plus Nathan and a few of his friends, but today she's taken a small table in the back corner of the cafeteria.

I'm still feeling a little bummed about getting detention, but I'm determined not to let it ruin my day. "What's up with the change in locale?" I ask, setting down my sack lunch.

"I'm trying to keep a low profile," she explains, fishing into her backpack. "I want to stay out of the public eye until this whole Geek Stink Breath thing blows over."

"Morgan! You're being paranoid. It's already blown over. It's not like anybody even saw it."

She shakes her head. "You don't know that for sure. Oh! I almost forgot." Morgan fishes in her backpack and then hands me a boxed set of *Alias* DVDs.

"Oh, thanks!" I place them in my bag. I can't wait to watch the show. I bet I'll pick up all kinds of excellent spy tips. Not that I've needed them thus far. Our bizarre meeting aside, Blaine's stay has been pretty uneventful. But I'll probably be seeing more of him soon, considering he's going to be starting school any day now.

"I've been meaning to ask you what the deal is with your mom's pregnancy. Did you find anything out?" Morgan takes a bite of her yogurt.

"Not yet." With all the Blaine excitement, I haven't gotten the chance to confront my parents yet. Truth is, I've been a bit preoccupied. "I guess I'll find out eventually." I take my turkey sandwich out and begin tearing it into little pieces. "How's your food?"

Morgan raises an eyebrow. "You don't seem too worried anymore. Was it a false alarm? What happened with all that business about the house being more crowded and stuff?" She stirs her yogurt with a plastic spoon.

Realization dawns on me, and I breathe a huge sigh of relief. "Oh, that's easy," I start to say, and then stop myself. Now it all makes sense. How could I have been so *dumb*? Mom isn't pregnant! She must have been talking about having Blaine stay with us. Some spy I am. I put two and two together and I get six. I can't figure out clues that are right under my nose.

Of course, there's still the issue of Dr. Gifford. . . . There's no way that could have anything to do with Blaine. For the life of me I can't think of a single reason why a *guy* would go visit an ob-gyn doc. Ick.

"What's easy?"

I scramble for something. "Mom just bought a bunch of new furniture," I lie, "and the house is going to be pretty crowded until we get rid of the old stuff."

Morgan scrunches up her mouth. "Uh . . . *okay*. No offense, but your parents are kind of odd sometimes."

"Sometimes?" I tease. "More like all the time." I take a sip of my bottled water.

She laughs. "I guess that's true of all parents."

"Puh-lease, your mom's like the coolest woman on the planet."

"Most of the time. Although she wasn't so cool with me going to the movies with Nathan Saturday. She wigged out completely when Nate suggested we see a late showing. Mom said I had to be home by eleven or else."

"That sucks," I agree.

Most days after school I go straight to the *Copperfield Courier* newsroom to put in an hour of work before heading home. But thanks to Mr. Clemmons I'm stuck in detention all week, which means my newspaper work will suffer. I suppose it's not fair to place all the blame on him. Much as it pains me to admit it, I got myself into this situation. I guess he was just doing his job. Although, did he really have to get so much joy out of seeing me suffer?

Detention isn't a picnic, but it's definitely not as bad as I expect. The crappy part is that you're not allowed to read or write, which means schoolwork is off limits. Sleeping is out, too. You basically have to sit there for an hour and stare off into space while watching the minutes tick by on the clock. I have never understood this. Most people wind up in detention for cutting class or not handing in their homework. The room is packed with kids who are barely pulling Ds. So if they want to spend their detention time studying, then shouldn't that be encouraged? This is a school, after all. Anything that brings up our grades is a good thing, right? But since I can't change the rules, I have to find other ways to kill time.

My plan is to spend the hour daydreaming about Scott Ryder, but before long my thoughts start drifting to Blaine Donovan. He's such a mystery. I know he's from Texas and that his father is, gulp, a billionaire, but other than that I know virtually nothing about him. I don't know what kind of music or movies or food he likes. I don't know if he has any hobbies. Geez, I don't even know his age! There are so many questions I want to ask. Does he play sports? Does he have a lot of friends back home? Does he have a *girl*friend?

I push that thought out of my head and

go back to dreaming about Scott Ryder. Before long the hour is up, and it's time to go home.

I walk in the front door around four o'clock and find Blaine camped out in front of the TV watching *Spider-Man 2*. Okay, so he likes action films. One question down, a million to go.

"Hi Kaitlyn!" he says, hitting pause on the DVD. "How was school today?"

"Not so great," I admit, setting down my backpack. "I was late to homeroom so I got stuck with detention for the week."

"Raw deal," he says. "You want something to drink? I was just going to get something from the kitchen."

"Sure." We make our way into the kitchen and Blaine opens the cabinet and takes out two glasses. "What would you like?" He opens the refrigerator and glances inside. "You have Coke, iced tea, orange juice—" He breaks off. "Why am I telling you this? You probably already know!"

I laugh. "Here, let me." I walk over and attempt to take the glasses from him. "You're our guest. *I* should be fixing *you* a drink, not the other way around."

"Nonsense! You've had a rough day. I, on the other hand, have been sittin' on my butt all afternoon. Let me take care of you." I start to object, but he cuts me off. "No arguments, you got it?"

Wow, he's so polite. I wonder if he's feeling a little stir-crazy after being cooped up in the house for three straight days. "I'll have a Coke," I tell him.

Blaine fixes my drink and then pours some iced tea for himself. "Here you go," he says, handing me the glass of Coke.

"Thanks." I plop down at the breakfast table and Blaine sits across from me.

"So you work for the school newspaper," he says.

"Yeah, how'd you know?"

He dumps a few sugar packets in his tea. "Your mom showed me some back issues this morning after breakfast. She saves all your old newspaper clippings."

She does? I never realized that. Mom has never seemed superexcited about my journalism work—at least not openly. This has always kind of puzzled me, since I thought she'd be happy that I was following in her footsteps. Not that I'm ever going to write about thongs and toe-curling kisses. Never,

ever, *ever*. It's not that I don't have any experience with them. Well, okay, the *real* reason is I've never wanted to wear a thong in my life. Morgan tried one out last summer when we went to Nathan's end of summer cookout. She spent the whole day walking around like there was a stick shoved up her butt. Thanks, but no thanks. And as for the toe-curling kisses . . . not so much. My ex-boyfriend, Jared, was completely obsessed with trying to get to second and third base. His kisses were all frantic and rough. Lots of lips, teeth, and rapid-fire tongue action. Ewwww. It's not a pleasant memory.

I must have a really horrible expression on my face, because Blaine immediately says, "Oh gosh, I hope it's okay that I read your articles. I didn't mean to pry."

"No, I think it's cool that you did that," I say, taking a sip of my drink. "Most of my friends don't even read my stories anymore. I'm glad you liked them."

"You've got real talent," Blaine says, downing his iced tea.

I figure this is as decent an opening as any, so I ask, "What kind of stuff do you like to do? Are you a writer?"

He shakes his head. "No. I've never

been very good at it. But I love to read."

"What else do you like to do?"

Blaine leans back in his chair and his eyes get a faraway look in them. "Pretty much anything outdoors. Horseback riding. Water skiing. Hiking. Surfing."

"Surfing?" I ask, giggling. "In Texas?" I've never been to Texas, but I've always pictured it being full of dude ranches, cacti, and rodeos. Surfing doesn't fit with my image.

"Oh, yeah, there's lots of places to surf down on the Gulf Coast. But I never really go there. I like to surf in Big Sur when my family goes to California."

I take another sip of my drink. "How often do you go?"

"About a dozen times a year. We have a house there."

"That must be great to travel so much. I bet you rack up tons of frequent flyer miles."

"We actually have our own plane," Blaine tells me and then, suddenly, he looks bummed out.

Great. I should never have asked about his family. It's obviously a sad topic. I quickly change the subject. "By the way, I was sort of wondering . . . how old are you?"

"I turned seventeen last November."

"Hey!" I snap my fingers. "My birthday's in November, too! When were you born?"

"My birthday is the twenty-fourth," Blaine says.

"You're a Sagittarius," I say. "So am I. I was born on the thirtieth." So we share a zodiac sign. I have to admit I think this is pretty cool.

"Well, what do you know?" He flashes me another toothpaste-perfect smile. "Although that zodiac stuff is kinda lame, don't you think? Kid stuff."

I blush. Does that mean Blaine thinks I'm just a kid? I am a whole year younger than him, after all. But before I can think of an answer, I hear the back door opening, and I instantly tense up. It's nowhere near five o'clock yet. Dad won't be home for at least a half hour and Mom never gets back before six. I try to steady my nerves, but my heart is racing. Why oh why didn't I study up on some spy techniques? What if this is some crazed madman coming to kidnap Blaine! What if . . .

"Hello! You guys down here?"

"Dad?" I ask tentatively.

He appears in the kitchen doorway. "Hi,

gang." He turns to Blaine. "I've got some great news for you."

"Did you catch the people who are after me and my family?" Blaine asks eagerly.

"Sorry." Dad's face falls. "I oversold it. My news isn't that good." He sets down his briefcase on the kitchen counter and takes out a large envelope. "Your paperwork was completed today. I've got your new license and documentation. And I've already spoken with the principal at Copperfield High, so they should have everything ready for you to start classes this Friday!"

Nobody says anything for a minute, so I jump in. "Blaine has to start classes on a Friday? That's unbelievably lame! Can't they let him wait until next Monday so he can enjoy his weekend?"

"I pressed to get this through as quickly as possible," Dad says. "The sooner we get Gordon's cover established, the better."

Blaine and I both stare at him. "Who's Gordon?" I finally ask.

"This man right here," Dad says walking over and placing his hand on Blaine's shoulder. "For the rest of your stay in St. Louis, you'll be known as Gordon Dennis Nichols!" he announces triumphantly.

Eight

I stifle a laugh.

Um, Gordon Dennis Nichols? Who thought *that* up? Does Blaine's "cover" also say he's a major geek? "Why Gordon?" I ask my dad. What I really want to say is, "What's wrong with the FBI? Couldn't they give him a nice, normal name like David or Michael instead of a nerdy name like Gordon? Are they *trying* to screw up his social life?"

Dad shrugs. "I don't make those kinds of decisions. It's really not that important. This is merely a temporary thing while the investigation continues. It's not like Blaine has to be Gordon for the rest of his life. In fact, you could even have a nickname," Dad offers, running his fingers through his almost nonexistent hair. "Like Gordy or Gordo."

"Gordo?!" I exclaim. "I hate to tell you, Dad, but that's beyond dorky."

Before we can argue on it further, Blaine pipes up. "It's okay. I think I'll stick with Gordon. Thank you, sir." He picks up the new driver's license and turns it over in his hands. "What's in a name?" he jokes.

"You're going to fit right in, Gordon." Dad looks so proud of himself, which is kind of ironic. This whole thing is borderline ridiculous, seeing as how a hottie like Blaine/Gordon could never go unnoticed at Cop-a-Feel High. He's going to be the center of attention the second he steps through the front door. I don't tell Dad that, though. He's got this mondo excited look on his face, and I don't want to burst his bubble.

"The paperwork says you're from Peach Tree City, Georgia, which is right outside of Atlanta. We had to go with somewhere southern so your accent would ring true, but we wanted to get away from Texas."

Blaine nods. "Georgia's great. I can easily pretend to be from there."

"One other thing," Dad says, turning to

face me. "Gordon is going to be posing as your third cousin. And since his last name is Nichols, he's from my side of the family. So if anyone asks, that means you and Gordon share the same great-great-grandfather. Got it?"

I nod, even though I don't have a clue how this bizarro family tree works. I have never understood all those second and third cousin things. At least Dad hasn't added a "once or twice removed" to the mix. Then I'd really be lost.

"Your mom will be home in an hour or so, and I was thinking we could all go out for dinner tonight to celebrate Gordon's arrival. What do you say?"

I absolutely love going out to eat, so naturally I say yes. Blaine is excited, too. "Where are we going?" Blaine asks.

"How about The Cheesecake Factory?" Dad says.

The Cheesecake Factory is practically my favorite restaurant in the world. Their dinner portions are so ginormous that I'm always stuffed by the time dessert rolls around. Still, I always have to order a piece of white chocolate raspberry truffle cheese-cake even though I usually throw in the towel after a bite or two.

"The Cheesecake Factory would be divine!" I say.

"What do you think, Gordon?" Geez, Dad is really taking to this whole Gordon thing.

"I've never been—never heard of the place, to tell you the truth—but I love cheesecake, so I'm game."

How can Blaine's family own a private plane but he's never heard of The Cheesecake Factory?

"Why don't you and Gordon go get ready?" Dad says. "We can leave as soon as your mom gets home."

I want to wear a skirt or dress to dinner, which requires freshly shaven legs, so my first stop is the bathtub. When I'm finished, I go to my room to pick an outfit. I spend eons looking through my closet, finally settling on a short black skirt, a tight burgundy top from Express, and a pair of knee-high black boots. It's one of the chicest outfits I own, and I always feel super self-confident when I'm wearing it.

I take great pains getting dressed and fixing my hair and makeup. I flatiron my frizzies until they're sleek, and I curl my eyelashes and carefully apply liner and eye shadow. It takes nearly an hour, but when I'm finished, I'm pleasantly surprised with the final product. Maybe I should start getting up an hour earlier for school and do this every day!

I don't know why, but I'm really excited about dinner. It's going to be so fun to take Blaine out and show him off—even if it's only to other diners in the restaurant. I'm feeling pretty fantastic until I get downstairs and bump into Mom. She's sitting on the living room couch chatting with Blaine/Gordon.

"Kaitlyn!" she says when she sees me. "You look adorable!"

Adorable? I was so not going for adorable. Sex goddess, maybe. Gorgeous, even. Heck, I'd have been satisfied with a simple "You look really nice." But "adorable" makes me sound like a kindergartner.

Then Mom says, "The last time you dressed up like this was your first date with Jared, wasn't it?"

I gasp. Oh my God, why did she have to bring that up? Now Blaine's eyeing me curiously. He probably thinks I consider this some whacked-out double date with him and my parents. I'm so humiliated.

Luckily, Mom gets up from the couch. "Let me go change clothes and then we can leave."

I start to sit down next to Blaine, being careful to leave an empty seat between us. But my heel gets caught on a loose strand of carpet and I fall into the middle seat, practically landing in his lap.

"Uh, sorry," I mumble, quickly scooting over to the opposite end of the couch. I certainly don't want to make this any more awkward. Blaine keeps looking at me in this funny way, and I worry he's about to set me straight. What if my crush is totally obvious? Not that what I have is a crush. Not exactly. It's more like a precrush. There should be some term for that.

"I was wondering if I could ask you something?" Blaine says shyly.

I nod. Uh-oh, here it comes.

"Who's Jared? Your boyfriend?"

Whoa. This could be a good sign, right? I try to steady my nerves. "He's my ex-boyfriend. We broke up a while ago. He transferred to a private school a couple of months ago, which made things easier. Now I don't have to see him between classes or at pep rallies and games."

Blaine thinks it over. "Do you still hang out with him?"

"Never. We broke up on kind of bad terms." I examine Blaine's face for some reaction—relief, happiness—but nothing shows.

"I'm sorry to hear that. People suck sometimes," he says, pushing a lock of hair out of his eyes. "And bad breakups especially. It's the same way with my ex-girlfriend, Keri. She cheated on me, and there was no way I was gonna stay with her after that. At first I was really depressed, but then I realized it was better to find out her true personality now."

I can't imagine why any girl in her right mind would cheat on a guy like Blaine. "For what it's worth, I think this Keri girl is an idiot."

"Thanks." He smiles. "Do you have a lot of guy friends?"

"A few," I say, although this is kind of a stretch. Other than Morgan's boyfriend Nathan, I don't have any guy friends. And Nate and I are only friends by default, because he's my BFF's main squeeze. I'm dying to know what Blaine means by all this, so I just come right out and ask. "Why are you so interested in my guy friends?" This is a little bold for me. I'm usually not so brave, but I figure that bravery is a crucial trait for a junior spy.

"I was thinkin' how hard it's going to be to meet people," Blaine says. "I figured if you knew a lot of guys, you could help introduce me around."

"Oh." I feel stupid now. Duh, of course that's what he meant.

"Unless you like shooting hoops and stuff," Blaine continues. "And, uh, I'm a sucker for air hockey."

I smile. "I'm not much of a basketball player, but I'm practically the state champ when it comes to air hockey."

Blaine's eyes twinkle. "Well, you may be the Missouri state champ, but I got Texas all the way."

"Is that a challenge?" I tease.

"Might be." He smiles. "What do you say we have a face-off one of these days?"

"It sounds like a plan."

Blaine extends his hand and we shake on it. Even though it's brief, it feels funny touching him. We talk for a few more minutes about our upcoming air hockey date (well, maybe "date" is the wrong word), and then my parents come downstairs and we leave for dinner.

"Oops, I almost forgot something," Blaine says, dashing upstairs to retrieve a gray North Face jacket.

"Great jacket," I tell him, admiringly.

"*This* thing?" he laughs, slipping it on. "It's okay . . . I mean, my family wouldn't let me bring any of my really nice clothes, so I had to settle for stuff like this."

Settle for North Face? Is he kidding? I would kill for a North Face jacket! Before I have time to ask if he's joking, Dad ushers us out the front door.

I sit in the backseat next to Blaine during the car ride, but we don't talk much. My mom spends most of the trip telling us about how she got into a fight with her editor. "He doesn't understand that I want to take some time off, work from home a little more. Most of the other columnists are allowed to do it, so why not me?"

My ears perk up when she says this. What possible reason would Mom have to want to work from home unless she, gulp, really is pregnant?

Even on a Monday night, The Cheesecake Factory is packed. We have to wait half an hour for a table. We finally get seated at a table right smack dab in the center of the restaurant, which suits me fine. I'm a people person by nature, and I love being at the center of the action. Although . . . this probably isn't the best vantage point for a spy. We're open targets, sitting ducks for anyone who wants to make a play for Blaine. I decide to keep my eyes peeled for anything suspicious. I'm sure Dad is doing the same thing but when I look over at him, he's happily browsing through the menu, oblivious to what's going on around us.

"So, Blaine, what kind of food do you like?" Mom asks.

"Yes, *Gordon*, what are you going to order?" Dad says, shooting my mother a pointed look.

"Sorry," she whispers.

It's an easy mistake to make. This name thing is going to be tough!

"I guess I'll have pizza," Blaine decides. He looks kind of bored. "We never get pizza at home, so I might as well be adventurous."

"You never have pizza?" I ask. That seems so strange! I can't imagine life without pizza.

"I maybe have it once a year. Most of my friends would rather sit around the country club eating prime rib or lobster."

I can't imagine passing over pizza or burgers for something like lobster. Seafood is way gross, if you ask me. "I've never even tried lobster," I admit.

"What a shame." Blaine laughs. "You're missing out."

I feel my face redden. He looks so amused, like he can't believe there's someone on the planet who has yet to try lobster. Wow, I realize suddenly, this must seem positively pedestrian to a guy like Blaine. He's used to fancy restaurants, lobster dinners, expensive clothes. I'm sure being around dull, ordinary, uncultured people like me must bore him to tears! He's probably just being nice to me because he has to.

The waiter comes over and I order lemon chicken with mashed potatoes, and both Dad and Mom get pasta. True to his word, Blaine orders the Big Five Pizza, which is an enormous pie covered with pepperoni, sausage, mushrooms, and peppers. He asks them to hold the onions, which is what I always do if I think I'm going to be kissing someone soon.

Dinner is really pleasant and when it comes time to order dessert I'm surprised to find Blaine and I like the exact same type. "You want to share?" I ask. "I can never eat a whole piece."

"Sounds good," he says, shrugging. I blush again. Why do I have to be so pushy? He probably wants his own piece but is too polite to say so.

We've just gotten our desserts when I feel somebody squeeze my shoulder. It startles me and I accidentally drop my knife, sending a sliver of cheesecake tumbling to my lap. "Well, hello there, Kaitlyn."

I turn around to see who it is. Oh. My. God. Of all the people in the world did we have to run into Amber Hamilton?! Talk about spoiling your appetite.

"Who's your friend?" she asks, gesturing toward Blaine.

"Oh, this is my cousin Gordon," I say.

"Cousin." She giggles. "I should have known. Not that you two look alike but, well, *you know*."

I hate her. I absolutely hate her. I want to stab her with my butter knife.

"Aren't you going to introduce me to everyone?"

"Mom, Dad, Gordon, this is Amber Hamilton. We go to school together."

"Gordon's going to be at Copperfield High soon," Dad announces.

Amber's eyes grow huge, but she quickly recovers. She tosses her long red hair over one shoulder. "So nice to meet you." She smiles briefly at my parents, but then her attention goes right back to Blaine. "Gordon, are you from out of town?"

"I just moved here from Georgia," Blaine says.

"Georgia!" Amber squeals. "So that's where your accent comes from. Has anyone ever told you how precious it is?" Before Blaine can answer she turns and gives me an exaggerated nudge. "He's a cutie. You should have introduced us before now. Kaitlyn, you're one of my best friends and I didn't even know you had a hottie cousin!"

Could she lay it on any thicker? Amber's going to need a shovel to get out from under all this. Surely no one is buying this.

"I like your friend," Dad says after Amber has walked away to go rejoin her family.

Dad's a secret agent—he should be a better judge of character than this. I want to tell him the truth about Amber, but I don't want to come off as a jealous wench in front of Blaine.

My mom, who has been quiet this whole time, throws me a knowing look. "It's a girl thing," she mouths, and I think she's right. Some things guys just don't understand. And girl-to-girl bitchiness is one of them. They never get when we're being fake with each other.

"She seems very nice," Dad adds.

I'm about to object when I look over and see Blaine nodding his head. "Just when I was worried St. Louis might not be so great, things are starting to look up. Especially if all of Kaitlyn's friends are so awesome."

I feel my heart sink. He thinks Amber is awesome?

"I'm glad you're getting a jump-start on meeting people," Dad chimes in. "Who knows, maybe Gordon and Amber will become great friends. Wouldn't that be terrific, Kaitlyn?"

"Yeah," I say, stabbing at my cheesecake with a fork. "Abso-*freaking*-lutely terrific."

Nine

Dad lets me drive us home from the restaurant. This is a rare treat. He almost *never* lets me drive his car, which is a really nice silver Acura. Even when we had driving lessons, he made me practice on Mom's SUV. But I can tell Dad is in a fantastic mood tonight. Dinner went really well, and we even got the chance to introduce "Gordon" to one of my classmates.

At the thought of Amber, my mood sours. I swear, sometimes I think that girl is out to ruin my life.

I unlock the car and climb into the driver's seat. Blaine sits up front next to me, and Mom and Dad snuggle together in the back like newlyweds. My parents are so affectionate you would never know they've been married twenty years. It's a little nauseating. Blaine talks to me, though, and that takes my mind off Mom and Dad's cuddlefest.

"Dinner was nice," he says as I put the car in reverse and back out of the parking space.

"Yeah, it was." It's funny how Blaine pronounces the word *nice*. His accent makes the *i* sound three syllables long.

"So that was your mortal enemy," Blaine says.

"What? How do you know that?" I put the car in drive and steer out of the parking lot and onto the street.

"You told me the first day we met," he explains.

"I did?" I don't even remember this.

He laughs. "You did. So what's the deal with y'all? She seemed nice enough. But looks can be deceiving."

"It's a long story." I'm cruising slowly down the street when my mind flashes back to *The Ultimate Spy Manual*. I remember what it said: *When driving, take unusual routes and switch lanes often to avoid being followed.* Wow, I've really let my guard down. For all

I know we're being followed. I glance in the rearview mirror. A dark blue Toyota sedan is lumbering along slowly behind us. Immediately, I'm suspicious. Why hasn't the driver pulled around to pass us? I push down on the gas, testing the car's acceleration. Thank God, Dad doesn't seem to notice. He normally freaks when I drive fast. I take the car up to fifty miles an hour, and the Toyota matches my speed. Uh-oh, this isn't looking good. I decide to try and lose him.

"Someday you'll have to tell me what happened between you and Amber," Blaine continues.

"Yeah, when you've got ten hours to listen to the whole sordid story." I round the corner without slowing down. The Toyota follows close behind. My heart starts racing. Maybe I should tell Dad that I suspect we're being followed. He's the professional. He'll know what to do. But then I remember what Dad said the first day Blaine was here. Blaine's life is in *my* hands. If we're at school together and something creepy happens, I can't call Dad and get him to fix it. It's time I learn how to take care of these things by myself.

I abruptly switch lanes, moving from the right to the far left in one quick swerve. Finally, Dad notices that something is going on. "No need to floor it, Kaitlyn. This isn't a race."

"Yeah, let's get home in one piece," Mom chimes in.

Easy for them to say. They don't know what I'm up against. Despite my frantic driving, the Toyota is still clearly behind us. I'm not sure where to go from here. The turnoff for our street is in a couple blocks. If I take it, the Toyota can follow us right home. If, on the other hand, I keep going straight, Mom and Dad will definitely know something is up.

I decide to make one last attempt to lose the sedan. I switch lanes again and this time the Toyota doesn't follow. It turns left onto a side street and vanishes out of sight.

Whew. False alarm. But at least it gave me a good chance to practice my spy driving. And I think I did pretty well, thank you very much.

As we pull into the driveway, Blaine says, "You drive like you're in training."

"In training?" I gulp.

"Yeah, for the Indy 500," he snickers.

Harsh. But I don't want Blaine to know I thought we were being followed—it'd just make him worry—so I don't say anything.

We walk into the house. I'm about to make my way upstairs when Dad places his hand on my shoulder, holding me back. "Hang on a minute." Once Mom and Blaine are out of earshot, he says, "I saw it too."

"The car?"

He nods. "Four-door navy blue Toyota Camry, small dent in the back driver's-side door. Missouri tags."

"I didn't think you noticed," I say. "And I didn't want Blaine to worry."

"It was probably nothing."

"I was trying to lose him," I tell Dad.

"I know that, too." He smoothes a wrinkle from his green pastel shirt. "You did a pretty impressive job. But next time, try to be a little less obvious. You never want them to know you're on to them. It's possible the driver turned off the road because he realized he'd been caught."

This sends a shiver down my spine. I study Dad's face. He seems concerned. Suddenly, I'm terrified. "Oh, God, Dad, what if that guy was after Gordon?" I ask. Then something occurs to me. "How did you know the car had a Missouri tag? He never got in front of us. You couldn't have seen his license plate."

Dad reaches into his pants pocket and hands me a dry cleaning receipt. Scrawled at the bottom, in scraggly handwriting, is a license plate number.

I'm stunned. "How did you get this?"

"I noticed the Toyota when you were pulling out of the parking lot. It was one row over from us, and whoever was in the car was just sitting there in the dark, waiting. That caught my interest, so I made a mental note of the license plate, assuming I wouldn't need it. But when the car reappeared behind us on the road a few minutes later, I jotted it down so I wouldn't forget."

"I can't believe you knew to do that!" I'm really impressed. My dad makes being a spy look like a piece of cake.

Dad gives me a quick hug. "I can't believe *you* knew to lose the car. That was remarkable! As for keeping mental tabs on license plates, I do it all the time. Even before Gordon moved in. I'm always checking out our surroundings wherever we go."

This blows my mind. "You're joking, right?"

"Nope. Every dance recital. Every shopping trip. I'm always paying attention. You have to be on the lookout for suspicious things constantly—the FBI taught me that. Ninety-nine percent of the time it adds up to nothing. But you don't want to miss that one percent where it pans out. You have to be on your guard for that."

I lean back against the wall, letting this sink in. I feel really shaky.

Dad gives me a reassuring smile. "It'll be okay. I've got things under control. You just go upstairs and do your homework." He takes the receipt back from me. "I'm going to go run these plates. I'll let you know what I find."

Despite Dad's suggestion, I know I won't be able to concentrate on homework right now. I need to talk to somebody. I want to call Morgan, but she doesn't have a clue what's going on over here and she won't be able to offer much support.

I decide to go see how Gordon/Blaine is doing. I can't help thinking he's a nice guy, even if he is a teensy bit of a snob. But I guess that comes with the territory when you're the son of a billionaire.

Blaine is staying upstairs in the guest

room, which is at the opposite end of the hall from my bedroom. He almost never comes out of his room at night. I have no idea what he does in there. I tentatively knock on the door.

"Come in," he calls.

I step into the room and find Blaine sprawled out on the bed, reading a book. "Hi."

"Hey!" Blaine sets his book on the bed. He looks really surprised to see me.

"What are you reading?" I ask, coming over and sitting down on a chair facing the bed.

"*A Tale of Two Cities*," he says. "I had a paper on it due next week at my old school." He gets a far-off look in his eyes and then laughs. "I don't know why I'm bothering to finish. Guess I just want to know how the story turns out."

I pull my legs up and fold them underneath me in the chair. "When did you find out you had to leave?"

"About fifteen minutes before your dad showed up at the hotel."

"The hotel?"

Blaine nods. "Last week the FBI took me and my mom out of our house and put us in a hotel. I thought we would be going back home in a day or two. Then everything changed. The threats got more serious."

"Where is your mom?" I ask. "Did she get to go back home?"

Blaine shakes his head. "I don't know for sure, but I'm pretty sure she didn't. There were threats made toward her, too. The FBI split us up because they felt it was safer that way."

"You're safe here," I say.

He leans back against the headboard of the bed and sighs. "I hope so. Sometimes I worry—"

"Kaitlyn."

I jump a mile. "Oh, hi, Dad."

"I can help you with that algebra problem now." He gives me a pointed look.

"Thanks." I get up, even though there is no algebra problem. Dad must have news about the car. I'm dying to know what Blaine was about to say. Doesn't he think my dad can protect him? But it will have to wait. "Have a good night, Blai—Gordon," I catch myself.

"Night," he says, going back to his book.

Dad and I go into my room and he shuts

the door. "We have to stop meeting like this," I crack.

Dad chuckles, and I feel a little better. He wouldn't laugh if he had bad news, right? "I just finished running the license number."

I can barely contain myself. "And?"

"Everything's fine."

I breathe a huge sigh of relief and flop onto my bed. "Thank God!"

"The car is registered to Mrs. Regina Kimble, a seventy-three-year-old woman who lives over on Macon Crest, the exact same side street where the car turned off earlier. There was no stolen vehicle report but, just to be sure, I had one of my colleagues give Mrs. Kimble a call. Turns out her grandson took the car out earlier tonight and brought it back just a few minutes ago. She said he went out to dinner, but she didn't recall the name of the restaurant."

I feel a million times better. "Thanks, Dad." I would never admit this out loud, but it's kind of cool to see him in his element. All these years I've known my dad was an undercover agent, but I've never actually witnessed his skills in action.

"Finish up your homework and then get

to sleep," he advises. "You've had an event-
ful night."

"I will. I promise."

As soon as Dad is gone, I hop on
MySpace and write Morgan a message.

```
Hey girl,
You're never going to believe
this. But remember how my mom was
talking about the house getting
more crowded the other day? I
finally figured out what that
meant. My cousin, Gordon, is
coming to live with us for a
little while. . . .
```

I type out the whole story—well, the
fake version we're telling everyone. I'm a
decent liar, but Morgan is especially percep-
tive. She can almost always see through me.
The safest bet is to explain the whole thing
to her in an e-mail. That way she can't ask
any questions or poke any holes in what I'm
saying. The last thing I need is another
Laguna Beach nightmare.

I absolutely must tell Morgan tonight.
If Amber has her way, half the school will
know about Gordon by tomorrow morning.

I don't want Morgan to find out from anyone other than me.

Once I've sent the e-mail, I pick up my chemistry book and flip it open. For once, I'm looking forward to a night spent studying the periodic table. It's nice and boring. Just what I need.

Ten

The rest of the week goes by quickly. Between working at the *Copperfield Courier*, serving my detention hours, and buffing up on spy techniques, I'm swamped. Before I know it, Friday morning rolls around and Blaine/Gordon is about to start his first day at Cop-a-Feel.

I can't wait to get there and introduce him to everyone but, secretly, I'm nervous. What if no one buys that Blaine's my long-lost cousin Gordon? What if I slip up and call him by the wrong name? I've been practicing at home, but you never know. And even if I do everything right, there's no guarantee anyone will buy it. Suddenly, out of the blue, this megahottie cousin I've never talked about before shows up. Won't people think it's weird? Plus, Blaine and I look absolutely nothing alike. He's tall with straight black hair, brown eyes, and a medium complexion. I'm pale as a ghost with frizzy blonde curls, and even in platform shoes, I'm practically a midget. Not to mention the fact that Blaine is like a definite 9 or 9.5 on the hotness scale whereas I am probably closer to a 5.5.

My panic increases when I see Blaine waiting for me by the front door, backpack slung over his shoulder. I don't know how it's possible, but he's somehow gotten cuter since I last saw him, which was only about nine hours ago. He's dressed in loose jeans and a black button-down shirt, which he wears untucked. His dark hair keeps falling forward around his eyes. The girls are going to flip when they see him.

"You ready to go?" I ask, gathering my books together.

"I've been ready for an hour." He laughs. "I was so nervous I couldn't sleep."

"Trust me, Cop-a-Feel is nothing to get worked up over."

"Wait a second. Did you just call it Cop-a-Feel?" He bites his lip to keep from laughing.

I blush. "That's the, uh, unofficial name."

"Clever." Blaine turns to open the door. "I can't wait to get my schedule. I wonder if I'll have any classes with you."

We walk outside and head down the street toward the school. "You're a year ahead of me, so I doubt it. Juniors and sophomores never take English, science, or math together. But foreign language classes and things like drama and art are always mixed up."

Blaine strolls along beside me. "What language do you take?"

"French."

"Oh, I take AP German. At least, I did at my old school. Your dad said my—Gordon's—transcripts are pretty accurate. They wanted me to be placed in courses similar to the ones I had back home. Like they wouldn't want my transcripts to say I've taken advanced Japanese when I'm barely able to order sushi."

I laugh. "Ah, come on, all you need to know to order sushi is California roll and spicy shrimp roll."

"Mmm . . . I love California rolls. We should have sushi sometime," he says, probably just to be nice. A guy like Blaine wouldn't bother hanging out with someone like me unless he had to.

"Sounds like a plan," I say, but my stomach is going flippety-flop. The idea of sitting next to Blaine at a sushi bar makes me feel weak in the knees. Plus, I can see the school off in the distance, and I'm starting to get antsy.

As we cross the street, he says, "From the way your father talks, I might be here for the rest of the school year. He doesn't know how long the investigation will last."

"That's rough." I hoist my backpack farther up my shoulder.

"Oh, I'll get through it. On the bright side, this means I have enough time to make some new friends."

As we approach the building, we stop talking about the FBI and assume our new roles: Kaitlyn and Gordon Nichols, third cousins. We're having a fake chat about family reunions when Morgan spies us from down the street and comes running.

"There's my best friend," I tell Blaine.

"Which one is she?" he asks.

"The one in the blue shirt," I say. Morgan's being followed by three of her friends from the soccer team.

"Nichols!" she calls when she gets within shouting distance. Blaine and I wave back. Morgan can move fast, so a second later she's standing in front of us, not even out of breath. "So this is the famous Gordon Nichols!" she says, looking him up and down. Her jaw is practically on the floor. "Kaitlyn, you never told me your cousin was so . . . so . . ."

"Hot!" says Casey Freeburt, the goalie for the soccer team.

"Welcome to Cop-a-Feel!" Morgan says. "You're going to love it here." She laughs. "I know there are plenty of girls who will make sure of that!"

Blaine looks flattered, but kind of put off. "Um, hi, I'm Gordon," he says, extending his hand to Morgan. "Pleased to meet you." He turns to me. "Kaitlyn, can you show me where the office is?"

"We'll go with you!" Casey says.

"Oh, that's all right. I really don't need all this fanfare. Kaitlyn can show me." He starts toward the entrance. "Thanks for offering to help, though." And with that, Blaine and I head into the school, leaving Morgan and the other soccer girls standing there, stunned.

I deposit Blaine at the main office, where the assistant principal is waiting for him. "I'll see you later." He leans in and gives me a quick hug before walking into the office.

It feels awesome to touch him, but it confuses me. It wasn't a romantic hug at all. It was very friendly . . . cousinly, even. Of course. He has to act like we're chummy—we're supposed to have known each other our whole lives. Blaine's taking to this whole Gordon routine really well.

I look down at my watch. I still have more than ten minutes until homeroom. I could go back outside and find Morgan, but I don't much feel like talking. I trudge down the hall and into homeroom. Mr. Clemmons looks up when I come in.

"Ms. Nichols, nice to see you here so early."

"I'm making a conscious effort to be on time."

"Glad to hear it."

I sit down and start looking over my English notes for today's quiz. A few minutes later, students start trickling in. Two girls I've never talked to before stop and ask me about Blaine. They have all sorts of questions. *How old is he? Is he single? What kind of girls does he like?* I tell them seventeen, yes, and I don't know. The same thing continues through first, second, and third periods. By the time lunch rolls around, I'm on autopilot, spewing out answers before the questions are even asked. Everyone wants to know about Blaine.

And I'm starting to get irritable. Geez. Since when did everyone become so boy crazy? I know Blaine is hot, but you'd think my classmates had never seen a cute boy before. And there are plenty of cute guys here. Scott Ryder, for one. Why are all the girls so interested in Blaine? Why can't they go drool over Scott Ryder or something? Blaine doesn't need the attention. He's supposed to blend in, not cause a riot wherever he goes.

I join Morgan in the cafeteria, and I notice our lunch group has swelled. There are normally six of us who eat together. Now there are ten. I've just sat down when Blaine comes in. His eyes scan the room and land on me. He waves and begins heading over. He starts to sit by me when Amber Hamilton appears out of nowhere.

"Hi, Gordon. Why don't you come eat with us," she coos. "We've got plenty of space."

Blaine addresses me. "Kaitlyn, what do you think? Want to move over to Amber's table?"

I'm startled. I'm pretty sure Amber's invitation is for one. "Oh . . . that's okay. I usually sit here with Morgan," I say, giving him an out.

"Morgan can come, too," Blaine suggests.

"We kind of only have room for one more," Amber says sweetly, of course. I can see right through her. Luckily, so can Blaine, I think.

"You just said there was plenty of space," Blaine points out.

Caught, Amber begins to backpedal. "I guess we could squeeze a few extra chairs in. But I think we've only got room for you and Kaitlyn. The rest of *them*," she wrinkles her nose as she says this, "will have to stay here."

Blaine mulls it over for a second. "Nah, I think I'll stay here." He sits down across from me. "But thanks for the invite, Amber. That's awful friendly of you." I want to cheer. I can't believe he's just rejected her! I don't think that's ever happened before. Guys always fall all over Amber. But maybe

Blaine is tired of girls swooning over him. He's so handsome and rich, it must happen all the time.

Amber looks stunned, but she quickly recovers. "Oh, Gordon, that's so sweet of you to want to keep your cousin company. I'll just have to sit with you guys." She climbs into the chair next to Blaine. I want to lean across the table and slug her. I can't believe Amber! Why is she so pushy? Can't she take a hint?

Amber spends the entire lunch period leaning over Blaine while he eats. She's wearing a dangerously low-cut shirt, and her boobs keep threatening to pop out and smack him in the face. She talks a mile a minute, pumping Blaine for information. "What kind of house do your parents have in Georgia? Is it one of the gorgeous plantation homes? How long are you going to be staying in St. Louis? Do you like it here? Do you have a girlfriend? Are you into redheads?" But the worst is when she asks him if he has a date for Valentine's Day, even though it's nearly four weeks away! Blaine politely answers her questions, but he doesn't offer a lot of information about himself. The whole time Amber's talking, he seems very uncomfortable. I don't blame him. He has to maintain his cover. Making up stories about his "fake" life—growing up in Peach Tree City and playing for the boys' basketball team—has to be tiring. I'd never be able to keep it all straight.

"I didn't think I'd make it out of there alive!" Blaine whispers in my ear when we leave the lunchroom. "I was sweating bullets."

"I couldn't tell. You came off as totally calm, cool, and collected."

"Bye, sweetie," Amber says, coming up from the side and giving Blaine a peck on the cheek. "See you around."

"Not if I can help it," I mumble.

"What's that?" he asks, cocking his head to the side.

"Uh. I said, 'My, she's helpful.'"

"Uh huh," Blaine says, his eyes twinkling. "'Cause I could have sworn I heard something else."

Since I still have one day left of detention, Blaine waits for me after school in the library. He was planning to walk home by himself, but I suggested he hang around in the library until I finished. I felt awful doing it, but I want to follow Dad's orders.

I have to keep an eye on Blaine. I'm probably being paranoid. How much trouble could he get into walking home from school by himself? But after the whole Toyota scare the other night, I figure it's better safe than sorry.

I go find Blaine once I'm finished with detention.

"I'm sorry you had to stick around," I say when I get there.

He closes his precalculus book. "That's okay. I needed to get some homework done anyway. It's easier to concentrate here than at home."

"I have to stop by the *Courier* office and pick up my assignment for the next issue. You don't mind tagging along, do you?"

"Sure, no problem." Blaine stuffs his books into his backpack and we head out of the library. "I can't believe how far behind I am. By the time I get caught up, the school year will be over."

We walk down the hall and round the corner, heading toward the *Courier* office. "I'd offer to help, but I don't know if it would do any good. I'm probably not familiar with the subjects you're taking."

"Probably not. Thanks anyway."

I push open the door to the *Courier* office and Blaine follows me inside. "I'll be right back." I go over to my mailbox, which is located on the far wall of the newsroom. All the staffers have our own mailboxes and our managing editor, Miller, leaves notes and phone messages for us there. Since I had to miss the planning meeting Wednesday after school, I don't get any say in what my next story assignment will be. I'm worried I'll get stuck with the worst job ever. As it turns out, I'm right.

"Damn!" I mutter.

"Problem?"

I whirl around to find Scott Ryder standing behind me. "Oh, hi, Scott." I turn approximately ten shades of red. "I just got stuck with a crappy story assignment."

"Miller screwed you, too?" he asks, leaning over my arm to read. "New plumbing in the faculty bathroom. Ouch! That's rough. I got stuck covering the upcoming chess match."

I scratch my head. "Since when is chess considered a sport?"

"Since I missed Wednesday's staff meeting to take my car to the shop. Miller's getting revenge. He pulled rank and told me that if I couldn't bother to show up for meetings, then I couldn't handle the responsibilities of an editor. So he took over my section for the next issue."

I can't believe it! Scott Ryder and I are having an actual conversation that doesn't involve floppy disks or tobogganing. "What a jerk!"

"That's Miller for you. What'd you do to earn plumbing duty?"

I laugh. "I got stuck in detention so I missed the meeting, too. He said, 'If you can't be here to do your job, then I'll do it for you.' And he gave all the best features articles out to other staffers."

"That sucks. But why did you get detention? You don't seem like a detention type of girl."

Oh my God! So Scott has actually paid attention to my type? Before I can answer he glances down at his watch and says, "I gotta go. Hang in there, Kaitlyn. I bet you'll write the best damn plumbing piece this school has ever seen."

Scott leaves and I stand there, mouth agape. *He called me Kaitlyn.* Scott Ryder knows my name!

I glance up to see Blaine staring at me,

a weird look on his face. He's been watching me talk to Scott and when I meet his eyes, he looks away. For some strange reason, I feel guilty. Then I push that thought out of my head. It's silly to feel this way. I mean, it's not like Blaine is interested in me at all.

Is he?

Eleven

I am a terrible secret agent. I have virtually zero dedication. First sign of defeat and I throw in the towel. I stopped by the school library after lunch yesterday to see if they had any good spy books. Nada. I got way discouraged and let myself slack off. Now I'll have to work double time to catch up. When I get home from school on Friday, I'm pleased to see two red Netflix envelopes sitting in the mailbox. Yes! It's time to launch the next phase of my plan: spy movies.

I briefly debate making popcorn, but decide against it. I'll need both hands free to take notes and practice whatever cool spy moves I can pick up. I wave good-bye to

Blaine, then rush up to my room, taking the stairs two at a time. I put *The Bourne Identity* in the machine and hit play. In addition to being a fabulous way to learn, this is going to be a rocking good time. I grab a few clean pieces of paper from my English folder and prepare to take notes. I'm going to write down everything that happens. I can use all the help I can get.

When the opening scene rolls, I quickly forget about taking notes. Wow, Matt Damon sure is hot. Even with bullet holes in his back. Ew, they're deep-sea fishing and the boat is rocking so much. I would get way seasick. Now they're docking in a foreign country. Where is that? It looks like Italy, or maybe France.

I fast forward past a couple of slow scenes. Not that the movie is boring, but I really need to get to the spy parts. I finally slow it down in time to catch a scene of Matt kung fu chopping two police officers in a park. Now we're getting somewhere! That lightning-fast one-two punch thing he does looks pretty awesome. Knowing a move like that could sure come in handy if I need to protect Blaine. I know it's completely silly and far-fetched to take spy ideas from movies—and I highly doubt I'll ever use any of this stuff—but it looks like so much fun.

I back the DVD up and then go through the scene frame by frame. After I've watched it a couple times, I get up and try to mimic what he's doing. I pull two pillows off my bed and karate chop them, Matt Damon–style. Then I practice throwing them over my head and slamming them onto the ground. I'm midway through my attack when my bedroom door swings open. One of the pillows goes flying out of my hands and sails into Blaine's face.

"Oh, crap!" I shriek, rushing over to help him. "Are you okay?"

"I broke the golden rule," he says, lowering the pillow from his face to reveal a grin. "I snuck up on you while you were," he glances at the TV, "watching *The Bourne Identity*."

"Sorry. I was, um, doing some stretches."

Blaine leans back against the doorframe. "I was just wondering something."

I eye him quizzically. He seems really nervous. "Is everything all right?"

"Oh, sure. But I wanted to know—do you have Amber's e-mail address?"

"No, but she's on MySpace.com," I tell

him. "You can message her through there if you sign up."

He grins. "I used to love MySpace. But I took down my account a few weeks ago and I can't put a new one up."

"Too high profile?" I ask.

He nods. "Exactly. I don't want to splash my name and face all over the Internet. All I would need is for some of my old friends from Texas to see my picture listed next to the name Gordon Nichols."

"Good thinking." I pause. "I could message Amber on my account if you want. Ask her to call you or something." Secretly, I'm hoping he doesn't take me up on the offer.

"That'd be great!" he says, smiling.

I want to ask why he needs to talk to her, but I stop myself. Isn't it obvious? He probably wants to ask her out. I feel deflated, but I try my best to hide it.

"Anyway, I'll let you get back to your movie," Blaine says, glancing at the screen. "I've heard it's really good."

"You can watch it with me," I say. "You know, if you want to. . . ."

"Sounds fun." Blaine sits down on the edge of my bed. "Can you catch me up on the plot so far?"

I briefly fill him in as best I can on what's been happening, then unpause the DVD.

I don't know why, but I feel really awkward all of a sudden. It's not every day I have a boy in my room. In fact, the last time was . . . never. Mom and Dad have always had a rule against it. Despite how much they liked Jared, they wouldn't even let him up here. Which is probably a good thing. Jared was a huge horndog when we were hanging out at the movies or downstairs on the couch. If we'd spent any time alone in my bedroom, I might have gone a few bases further than I wanted to.

I sit down next to Blaine. He scoots back on the bed until he's leaning against the headboard. "I've always wanted to see this. But I don't get to go to the movies much back home."

Right, I think, *of course he doesn't.* Blaine's probably too busy hanging out at country clubs or vacationing on friends' yachts.

We watch the movie in silence for a while. Every now and then one of us cracks a joke or comments quickly on the plot. Whenever someone is speaking German, Blaine translates for me.

Blaine seems to be enjoying himself. And despite it being weird having this boy in my room, it really does feel so normal hanging out with him like this. There's no way my parents can object since they're the ones who brought him in the house in the first place.

Somewhere around the big car chase scene, I move back until I'm sitting right beside Blaine at the top of the bed. It's much more comfortable back here, even if it gives me butterflies being this close to him.

The longer the movie goes on, the more I realize what a crappy spy I am. Matt Damon's character can run ridiculously fast, even at high altitudes, whereas I suck at running. He's also really good at stunt driving and handling weapons. But no matter how hard I try to focus on the secret agent part of the movie, I keep getting distracted by the love story.

I can't help thinking how sexy it is when Matt Damon kisses the German girl—he's totally passionate—and how much I wish someone would kiss *me* like that. I glance over at Blaine briefly and, right at that exact moment, he looks over at me! We make eye contact for a nanosecond, then quickly turn away. Then Matt and the girl start making out and I feel a hot blush creeping up the back of my neck. Whoa, this is getting heavy! Thankfully, they cut the scene a second later.

My dad comes home with Chinese takeout right around the time we finish watching *The Bourne Identity*. After we eat, Blaine goes up to the guest room to work on his homework and I head to my bedroom to watch James Bond. My original plan was to watch the entire James Bond series, but the Pierce Brosnan movies are the only ones I can handle. Even still, 007 doesn't offer me anything useful. Bond spends half the movie making out with chicks and the other half using complicated gadget thingies that I can't get my hands on.

All in all, I don't enjoy Bond that much. I'm not sure if it's the actual movie or if it's because I can't get my mind off Blaine. I keep wishing we were watching it together.

Morgan calls later that night. It's just turned ten-thirty p.m. and I'm getting ready for bed. I tuck the Winnie the Pooh phone under my ear and proceed to change into my pajamas while we talk. But Winnie, in addition to looking a bit childish, is very difficult to balance under my ear. I keep dropping the phone on the floor and having to pick it back up.

"Do you want to spend the night tomorrow?" she asks.

"I can't," I tell her. I kick off my shoes and throw them in a pile in the corner.

"Come on, Nichols. You already canceled our standard Friday afternoon Quiznos and mall trip because of detention. The least you can do is hang out with me tomorrow."

"I'm sorry, I really can't. My dad insisted I stick around the house. Family stuff," I say. This isn't exactly one hundred percent true. Dad did suggest it would be good if I spent some time with Blaine this weekend, but he never insisted.

"Speaking of family, your cousin Gordon is freaking awesome!" she says. "When you e-mailed me about him you neglected to mention the most important part."

"Which is?" I ask.

"That he's—"

The phone slips out from under my ear again. "Dang it!" I lean down and pick it up. "Sorry, Morgan, I didn't catch any of that. I dropped the phone."

"I was just talking about how fine

Gordon is. He looks like a movie star."

"Yeah, he looks like Orlando Bloom," I say, struggling to keep Winnie in place.

"You're right, he does! Oh my gosh, he looks *exactly* like Orlando. Nichols, you are so lucky to be living in a house with a guy like him. I would just sit and stare at him all day."

Don't I know it! But of course I don't say this out loud. "Uh, gross, he's my *cousin*. Remember?"

"But he's not a first cousin, right?"

"Third." I reach into my dresser and pull out my pj's.

"So he's practically a nonrelative."

Take out the practically and you've got it right. "I don't care how far along he is on the family tree," I say, laughing. "A relative is a relative. That's disgusting."

"Then let me at him!"

"Morgan! What about your boyfriend?"

She giggles. "What boyfriend?"

"Nathan Haverhill. You know, your on-again off-again." I climb into my pajamas and toss my jeans and T-shirt in the hamper.

"Nathan, schmathan. I'd throw him on the back burner if it meant a shot with Gordon."

I put a hand on Winnie to hold him in place. "Are you serious? You'd really toss

Nathan out like yesterday's garbage for a quick hookup with Gordon?"

"No," she admits, sounding disappointed. "I'd never do that to Nate. I'm all talk, no action."

"That's not necessarily a bad thing. At least, not when it comes to cheating."

Morgan starts telling me all the details of her latest phone conversation with Nathan. While she talks I move over to my computer and log on to MySpace. I need to send Amber a quick note, like I promised Blaine. Before I can go to Amber's profile, I notice the blue *New Friends Requests!* icon on my screen. I quickly click on it.

"Oh . . . my . . . God!" I breathe.

"What?"

"Listen to this: Sports with Scott wants to be your friend!" I shriek.

"Huh? Who is Sports with Scott and why does he want to be my friend?"

"No, no, no . . . Morgan! I'm on MySpace right now and Scott Ryder just sent me a friend request!"

"Oh!" she squeals. "Yes! That's right, I forgot his screen name was Sports with Scott. He sent you a friend request?"

"Yes!"

"Nichols, that's awesome!"

I quickly hit accept. "This is too cool for words." I know I'm kind of a dork for being so excited, but I can't believe Scott took the time to look me up on MySpace. I scroll over to Amber's profile and send her a message.

Hi Amber,
This is Kaitlyn Nichols. My cousin, Gordon, wants you to call him when you get the chance.

I type out our phone number and click send.

"What are you typing?" Morgan asks. "Sending Scott a message?"

"Actually, I'm writing Amber Hamilton."

"Ew. Why?"

"Gordon asked me to."

"What, does he want to go out with her or something?"

"I guess so." I feel my mood sink again.

"Your cousin has bad taste."

"Apparently he does." The phone starts slipping again and when I grab it I accidentally bop myself in the chin. "Ow!" I moan, rubbing my face.

"Problem, Nichols?"

I flop back on the bed and kick out my legs. "It's this stupid phone. It's causing all kinds of problems."

"Yeah, what's up with that? I can't hear you at all."

"I'm talking on a really old plastic phone." I twirl the cord around my fingers. "Actually, it's a Winnie the Pooh phone from when I was five."

"Okay, two questions. One, why did you keep a baby phone and, two, why are you talking on it?"

"I don't know. Nostalgia?"

"I think that's enough nostalgia for one night," Morgan says. "Come on, switch it back."

I think it over. She's right, the connection on this thing is terrible. And it is really awkward to hold against my head.

Oh, to hell with it. "I'll call you right back," I say, and then I hang up and plug my cordless phone back in, vowing to switch back to Winnie the Pooh as soon as this conversation is over.

As soon as Morgan answers, I continue, "So, let's talk about Scott Ryder a little more. . . ."

Twelve

"Kaitlyn, there's someone here to see you," Mom calls up the stairs. It's Saturday afternoon and I'm sprawled out on my bed, paging through the latest issue of *Teen People* and daydreaming about Scott Ryder (I still can't believe he knows my name). I throw down the magazine and jog down the stairs.

It's probably Morgan. She seemed kind of peeved that I turned down her offer to hang out this weekend. She's probably stopping by to see if I've changed my mind. But when I reach the bottom of the stairs I realize I'm totally mistaken. It's not Morgan after all. In fact, it's . . .

I gasp.

Scott Ryder!

My knees buckle when I see him standing in the entrance hall. "Hey Scott!" I say, in what I hope is a friendly, laid-back tone. "What are you doing here?"

"Amber invited me. She's parking the car. She'll be in in a minute," he says, smiling brightly. "She wanted to surprise your cousin and asked me to come along."

"My cousin?" I repeat.

"Gordon," he says.

A second later Amber appears in the doorway behind Scott. "Hi Kaitlyn," she says, looking bored. "Where's Gordon? He's home, right?"

"Yeah, hold on. I'll go get him." I'm still in a state of shock. What are they doing here? Two weeks ago it would have been inconceivable that two of Cop-a-Feel's most popular kids would be in my house. Yet here they are.

I dash up the stairs and knock on Blaine's door. He doesn't answer, so I push the door open slightly and peek inside. No wonder he didn't hear. His back is to me and he's swaying back and forth, dancing awkwardly to the music on his iPod.

"Gordon," I say tentatively.

He keeps on dancing, shaking his head

from side to side. He opens his mouth and sings a few lines from a Coldplay song. His voice is terrible—really flat and off-key.

I place my hand over my mouth, stifling a giggle. I can't believe how silly he looks! I never would have imagined that suave guys like Blaine have goofy moments, too. I always thought people like him were born cool and that they never, ever faltered. I guess he *is* human, after all.

He closes his eyes and spins around twice, teetering back and forth as he goes. On his third spin he opens his eyes and catches sight of me. He's so startled he nearly topples over backward.

"Kaitlyn!" he cries, ripping the earphones off. He quickly turns off his iPod. "Oh my God! How long have you been standing there?"

"Long enough to catch most of your routine." I giggle.

His face turns a dozen shades of red. "Oh, no! I can get a little crazy when I listen to music sometimes," he groans. "I was dancing and everything, wasn't I?"

I nod.

"How completely *embarrassing*."

"No, it's cool. It was kind of . . . funny."

I almost say "cute" but stop myself just in time.

"Our little secret?" he asks hopefully.

"You can count on it."

"Thanks, Kaitlyn." He looks genuinely relieved.

"Anyway, we have some visitors downstairs."

"We do?"

"Yeah, Amber Hamilton and Scott Ryder are here."

Blaine runs his fingers through his dark hair, smoothing it into place. "I didn't know you invited them over."

"I didn't," I tell him, as we make our way out of the guest room and into the hall. "They just kind of showed up."

We head downstairs and into the living room, where Amber is sprawled out on the love seat. "Come join me, Gordon," she says, patting the empty space beside her. "I brought you a present."

I eye her suspiciously. She'd better not be giving him food. I don't mean to be paranoid, but the Ex-Lax incident springs to mind.

Blaine takes a seat next to her. "A present?" he asks, looking confused. "It's not my birthday or anything. . . ."

"Consider it a welcome gift," she coos, pulling out a bag. "Sort of. I'd really rather give you something a little more exciting. But we can work on that later."

I roll my eyes. Can she *be* any skankier?

Scott's just kind of standing around. "Have you got anything to drink?" he asks. "I'm parched."

"Oh, sorry!" I say. "I'm being way rude. Amber, Gordon, can I get you guys anything?"

"I'm fine," Amber says, not taking her eyes off Blaine.

"I'm good, too. Thanks, Kaitlyn." Blaine reaches inside the bag and pulls out a notebook. "Oh . . . thanks!" he says, looking a little bewildered. "Is it a journal?"

"No, silly, it's a German notebook. These are all my notes from Mrs. Kellerhouse's German class. When I talked to you on the phone the other night, you sounded so stressed about German class. I wanted to help out."

I feel my breath catch. They talked on the phone? I knew Blaine wanted her to call him—I sent the message on MySpace, after all—I just didn't realize Amber followed through.

"This way you can get caught up in no time. And I'd be happy to tutor you, if you want," Amber offers.

"That would be great, thanks!" Blaine looks really happy about Amber's gift.

Scott's still standing by my side. "I'd love a glass of Coke, if you've got it."

"Right, sorry," I say, drawing my attention away from Blaine and Amber. I head into the kitchen to get Scott a drink. He follows me.

"You have a nice house," he says, as I get out a glass and fill it with ice. "I didn't realize you lived over here. We're practically neighbors."

"Really?" I ask, pouring him some soda. "Where do you live?"

"On Bennett Lane."

I blink. "Bennett Lane? Wow, that's a really great neighborhood."

"Yeah, my dad does well," Scott says, taking the glass from my hands.

We stand there awkwardly. Our conversation seems to have run out of steam.

"You wanna go over some newspaper ideas?" he asks finally.

"We could do that," I agree. I start to walk back toward the living room.

Scott plops down at the kitchen table. "How about in here," he says. It's more of a statement than a question. "Give Amber and your cousin some alone time."

"Alone time?" I ask. "What is this, an episode of *The Bachelor*?"

"Something like that." He laughs. "Amber's really into the guy and you can tell he's way into her."

My eyes open wide. "You can?"

Scott nods. "Definitely. The way he looks at her . . . the boy's got it bad." He pauses. "Your cousin's really fitting in, Katie. With a girl like Amber by his side, he'll be cool in no time."

"I guess," I say. I can't help feeling a little uncomfortable with my dream guy here in the kitchen and my mortal enemy hanging out in the other room.

"Good deal," he says, flashing me his can't-miss smile.

He keeps calling me Katie. I wonder if that means anything? Nicknames are a form of endearment, right? I decide to go with the moment, to not second guess myself and see where it leads. Scott keeps looking at me, holding my gaze like we're great friends or . . . possibly more.

A guy like Scott Ryder would never be interested in me. But with the way he keeps acting, I can't help but wonder. We gossip about the newspaper staff and go over assignments for a while. The conversation is totally natural—Scott's an easy guy to talk to. I can see why he's so popular.

"Thanks for the MySpace add," I tell him, making conversation.

"Sure thing!" he says, flashing me a huge grin. "Your profile rocks, by the way."

I blush at the unexpected compliment. "Thanks."

We work on newspaper ideas for a while longer. Scott's an incredibly talented writer, and it's pretty great hanging out with him. He's so smart when it comes to journalism; bouncing ideas around with him has really helped me.

We head back into the living room an hour later and find Blaine and Amber hunched over the German textbook. Their heads are so close they're practically touching. Blaine looks like he's having an awesome time, like he's soaking up every minute that he's with Amber. I get a strange feeling in the pit of my stomach, but I push it away.

Despite having so much fun, I find myself wishing I'd spent the afternoon with Blaine instead of Scott.

Oh, God, what's happening to me! I can't like *him*. It's stupid, impractical, ridiculous. Blaine's my "cousin." He's out of my league. He probably wouldn't even give a girl like me the time of day, if it weren't for this whole my-dad-protecting-him thing.

Much as it pains me to admit it, I know I'm right.

Thirteen

"I got a weird e-mail today," Blaine says as we walk home from school Monday afternoon. "I wasn't sure if I should show it to you or not."

Alarm bells go off in my head. "What do you mean by weird?" I can't help but be suspicious. What if someone has tracked Blaine down in St. Louis? What if they've sent him a threatening letter?

He looks uncomfortable. "It was about you."

"Me?" I stop dead in my tracks. "What did it say?" I ask. "And who sent it?'

He chews on his lower lip. "That's the thing—I have no idea who sent it. It came in anonymously."

"How can an e-mail be sent anonymously? It has to show a return address, right?"

Blaine shakes his head. "That's what I thought, too. But apparently there's a way to go into Outlook and put in a fake return address. It's how people send spam and stuff."

"So what did it say?" I ask nervously. I can't imagine who would be writing to Blaine about me.

"It's not exactly good." He sighs. "Are you sure you want to know?"

Uh-oh. "Yeah, of course I'm sure." Although I'm actually not. I hate hearing people talk about me.

Blaine swallows hard. "I'm really sorry about this," he says, as he retrieves a folded up piece of paper from his pocket and hands it to me.

Dear Gordon,
Hope you're enjoying life at
Copperfield. Changing schools
is rough, even for a cool guy
like yourself. Right now you seem
to be fitting in, but I would
hate to see your social standing

tumble. And that's exactly what's gonna happen if you keep palling around with Caitlin Nichols. No offense, 'cos I know she's your relative and all. But she is a serious leech on your popularity. You haven't been at this school for long, so you probably don't realize what a loser she is. Let me fill you in: Caitlin is a major outcast. She is on the shit list at Copperfield—literally. She crapped her pants at the soccer tryouts a few weeks ago and people are still talking about it. Caitlin is a hanger-on who tries to fit in and fails miserably. Most of us feel really sorry for her because she's so damn oblivious to how lame she is. Caitlin doesn't get invited to parties or on dates. And I would hate to see that same sad fate befall you.

I don't wanna be a hater, but I just thought you should know.

—A Concerned Friend

I scrunch up the e-mail in my fist. I'm so furious I'm physically shaking. "That bitch! Never mind all the 'Kaitlyn's a loser talk.' I can handle that. That's just her dumb opinion. But she's making up lies! I'm not a hanger-on. AND I DID NOT CRAP MY PANTS AT THE SOCCER TRYOUTS!" I scream.

"Kaitlyn, calm down. It's okay . . ."

"No, you don't understand, Blai— Gordon," I say, catching myself in the nick of time. "She's lying! I didn't even *go out* for the soccer team. That was Morgan who that happened to. That bitch Amber needs to get her facts straight. God, you'd think she'd remember, seeing as how she's the one who spiked Morgan's Gatorade with laxatives and all."

Blaine looks confused. "Wait a minute." He holds up his hand to stop me. "Why are you mad at Amber? She's not the one who sent the e-mail."

"Of course she is!" I thunder.

"Amber's your friend. She wouldn't say these things."

Why is he defending her? "My friend? Puh-lease! She hates my guts. And, trust me, the feeling is mutual."

"I feel really bad about this, Kaitlyn, I really do. But you can't jump to conclusions," Blaine says. "I want to know who did this as badly as you do. And as soon as I figure it out, trust me, I'll let 'em have it!"

"Figure it out?" I sputter, unable to control myself. "There's nothing to figure out. It's Amber. Look," I say, waving the piece of paper in the air. "Look at how she spelled 'Caitlin.' That's classic Amber. When she wrote that crap about my dad being gay, she spelled my name with a *C*, too."

Blaine's eyes widen. "Your dad is gay?" he gasps. "But he's married! What about your mom?"

"Oh, no, no, he's not," I say. I quickly explain the CAITLIN'S DAD IS A FLAMER incident. "This is totally her style."

Blaine thinks it over. I can tell he's getting it, seeing through Amber's facade. And then he says, "But you don't know that. I agree that whoever wrote that on the blackboard is probably the same person who sent the e-mail. But you have no way of knowing that it was Amber who wrote on the blackboard in the first place. Do you?"

"It *was* her," I say confidently. "I heard

her friends laughing about it the next day, saying how brilliant Amber was for calling out my dad like that."

Blaine starts to object, but I cut him off. "Let's not talk about it," I say. "We're never going to see eye-to-eye. I'm just going to forget this whole e-mail even exists."

He looks like he wants to say something, but he doesn't.

"I'm gonna kick your butt tomorrow."

"You are not," I taunt, giving Blaine a wicked smile. "I already told you. I'm the air hockey champ of Missouri. You can't mess with that."

"Ah, yes. But you know what they say. Don't mess with Texas."

I groan. I walked right into that one.

It's later that night, and we're sitting sprawled out on the floor of the living room, watching *Smallville* reruns and trying to forget about the evil e-mail. Except we're not really watching the episodes so much as we're talking over them.

Things have been kind of tense between Blaine and me since our argument about the e-mail. But we're trying to move past it. We've made plans to go to the arcade after school tomorrow for our own personal air hockey tournament.

The phone rings. Ordinarily I would make a mad dash to answer it, but I'm so engrossed in *Smallville* that I let Dad get it.

A few minutes later he appears in the living room. "Gordon, it's for you."

I blink in surprise. What? How is that possible? Blaine jumps up and goes into the kitchen to get on the line.

"Dad!" I hiss, standing up off the floor. "Do you think that's a good idea?"

"Do I think what's a good idea?"

"Letting B—Gordon," I catch myself, "take a phone call. Are you sure it's safe? Remember what you told me the first day Gordon got here? You said if anybody called asking for him, that was an emergency."

"I said it was an emergency situation if anyone called asking for," he mouths the word, "Blaine. But you're right to be concerned. If anyone calls asking for Gordon, don't put him on the phone—take a message and bring it to me right away."

I feel like stamping my feet. I'm so annoyed. "No offense, Dad, but you're sending a ton of mixed messages. Can Gordon talk on the phone or not?"

"We're going to evaluate it on a call-by-call basis," Dad says, sounding all FBI-ish. "In this case, it's all right. It's just one of your friends."

"One of *my* friends?" I ask. "Morgan's calling to talk to Gordon?"

"Not Morgan. Amber."

"What?" I gasp. "YOU LET HIM TALK TO HER?!?!"

"Relax. She called here for him the other night, too. The girl is harmless. She wants to invite Blaine to a picnic tomorrow after school with some kids from Copperfield. I told her that sounded great and that Gordon would love to go."

"Since when are you making decisions for Gordon?"

Dad looks taken aback. I don't usually challenge him like this. "Since he's under my care, that's when. Amber and I talked for a couple of minutes and she mentioned the picnic tomorrow. I told her it sounded like a lot of fun and I was fairly certain Gordon was free."

I shake my head. "You don't get it. That girl is poison."

"Amber seems harmless. She's very friendly. It'll be good for Gordon to make some casual friends. As long as he doesn't get too close to anyone."

I feel like crap. "Gordon and I are supposed to play air hockey at the arcade tomorrow. We've been planning it all week."

Dad waves his hand dismissively. "One day apart won't kill you. It's important for Gordon to have a decent social life. It will help keep him from getting depressed. And," he whispers conspiratorially, "it's good for his cover. Sometimes the best place to blend in is the center of a crowd."

Dad leaves to go for his nightly jog, and I sink back down on the floor. My father has no idea what's he's talking about. Hanging out with Amber Hamilton isn't good for anybody, but especially not Blaine. He's probably feeling super vulnerable and weak right now. Amber will swoop in like a vulture and tear him to pieces.

Blaine comes back a minute later, looking embarrassed. "That was Amber," he says apologetically. "She kind of invited me to go to a picnic tomorrow with 'the girls.' It's at the same time as our air hockey tournament."

"I know. Dad told me."

"I feel awful about this. . . ."

He's going to cancel. He's going to cancel on me to go out with *her*. I pick at a stray thread on my jeans. I can't look him in the eyes. I don't want to give away how hurt I am.

"So I told Amber I couldn't go on account of our air hockey match," Blaine continues.

My ears perk up. He turned her down? To hang out with me? That's fantastic!

"And she said, 'That sounds fun, I love air hockey! The girls and I can meet you and Kaitlyn at the arcade. Unless there's some reason you *want* to be alone with your cousin.'"

I chew my lower lip. That doesn't sound good. Is it possible Amber's figured out Blaine's not my cousin? I push that thought out of my head. No, she's not that smart. She's just being bitchy.

"So I kind of had to say 'yes' after that," Blaine admits. "But I think it will probably be pretty fun. I hope you don't mind."

I do, but what can I say? "It's okay," I tell him. "I'll just kick Amber's butt after I kick yours!"

Fourteen

But it doesn't turn out that way. When we get to the arcade the following afternoon, Amber seizes control immediately. She's waiting by the front entrance wearing the least arcade-appropriate outfit imaginable— a tiny purple skirt that's barely bigger than a napkin, topped off with a black halter top. On her feet are a pair of tall black heels. She must have gone home to change while I was in the newsroom and Blaine was doing homework in the library. Amber looks like she's ready to go out clubbing. How is she going to play video games in that?

Amber swoops down on Blaine the instant we arrive.

"Hey, hon," she says, linking her arm

through his. "Want to beat me at skee-ball?" She's completely ignoring me. It's like I'm not even there.

"Kaitlyn and I came here to play air hockey," Blaine explains.

Amber doesn't quit. "You've got plenty of time for that. Skee-ball will get your arm warmed up." She rubs his biceps for emphasis.

Blaine gives her a polite smile. "Thanks, but Kaitlyn and I have a big air hockey tournament all planned out."

Amber finally acknowledges me. "You don't mind if I spend a few minutes alone with your cousin, do you, Katie?"

"We kinda had this planned." I study an invisible spot on my shoe. I don't want her to see how disappointed I am. Logically, there's no reason for me to be so territorial about my cousin. And I can't tell if Blaine genuinely wants to hang out with me, or if he's just being polite.

"I'm not going to ditch Kaitlyn," Blaine says firmly. "We came here together."

"Scott can hang out with her," Amber says.

Scott? What? I look up just in time to see Scott Ryder making his way over toward us. He's carrying a small cardboard tray with four drinks on it. "What are you doing here?" I blurt out.

"Amber invited me." He hands me a paper cup of Sprite, then continues passing the drinks around.

"I thought this was a day out with 'the girls.' Where are Kayla and Erica?" I ask.

Amber sips her drink. "Oh, they canceled at the last minute, so I called Scott."

"How's your plumbing piece going?" Scott asks, turning to face me. "I'm having hell with the chess team."

Seeing her opening, Amber links arms with Blaine again. "While you guys talk work, Gordon and I are going over here to *play*."

Blaine shoots me a "I hope this is all right" look. "It's okay," I tell him, a funny feeling forming in the pit of my stomach. "We can have our air hockey game later."

"I'll be back in a few minutes," he promises, following Amber over to the skee-ball machines. As I watch them go, I'm racked with confusion. Why do I feel so glum? I'm alone with Scott Ryder. I'm practically on a double date with him! This is the moment I've dreamed about for nearly two years. Why am I not more excited?

"So, how's that story coming?" Scott asks again, leaning against the side of a Whack-a-mole machine.

"Pretty good. Those tips you gave me really helped."

"I'm glad," he says. "You're a fantastic writer, Kaitlyn. Your work shows real promise."

"Thanks." I drink a little more of my Sprite. "That means a lot coming from you."

Scott pats me lightly on the arm. "Anytime." We talk about work for a few minutes, and then he pauses and looks around. "So, what do you want to do?"

I steal a sideways glance at Blaine and Amber. They're playing foosball and laughing and talking like old friends. He seems really happy to be with Amber—like he doesn't miss me at all. "How about air hockey?" I ask. That'll show Blaine. Plus, the air hockey tables are right next to foosball.

"No offense, but air hockey is kind of lame," Scott says. "*Arcades* are kind of lame," he adds, making a face. "Are you hungry?" he asks.

I blush. "Uh, yeah. I could go for some food."

"Come on, let's get something decent for lunch." He leads the way to Blaine and Amber. "Gordon, Amber, you guys want to grab some lunch? There's a phenomenal pizza place down the street."

Amber stops playing mid-foosball. "Yeah, that sounds fabulous. What do you say, Gordy?"

Gordy? Oh, God. It looks like Dad's lame nickname is starting to stick.

"What about air hockey?" Blaine asks. "You and I have only been playing for about ten minutes. And Kaitlyn and I *still* haven't gotten to play."

"We can come back here after lunch," Scott suggests. "Let's just go get some food."

"I guess I could go for a bite," Blaine says. "That okay with you, Kaitlyn?"

I nod. A few minutes later we all pile into Scott's Jeep—Amber and Blaine in the backseat, me and Scott up front—and cruise down to Pike's Pizza. We snag a big booth in the back of the restaurant. I slide into the far seat and Blaine climbs in behind me, cutting Scott off.

"Don't you want to sit by me, Gordy?" Amber purrs.

"Oh, sure!" Blaine says, hopping up. "Scott, you take this seat and I'll sit by Amber."

We settle into the booth. Despite my frustration with Amber, I am ecstatic. I cannot believe I'm sitting next to Scott Ryder! My heart is beating about a million times a second.

"So, what kind of pizza do y'all want to get?" Blaine asks.

"Y'all!" Amber exclaims, grazing Blaine's hand with hers. "That's soooo cute! I love your Georgia-boy accent. It's so sexy."

"Uh, thanks." Blaine moves his hand away from hers and picks up the menu. "How about pepperoni and mushrooms?"

"Great," I tell him. We decide to split two medium pizzas and get a pitcher of Coke.

"Did I tell you guys Erica and I are going to Cancun over spring break?" Amber asks. "It's gonna rock. You guys should come."

"Can't. I'm going to Panama City with my older bro," Scott says.

"What about you, Gordy?"

"Gee, thanks, Amber," he says. "But that's not really my scene."

"Not much of a traveler?" Scott says knowingly. "I used to be that way, too. But then we started flying first class. So much better. You ought to try it, Gordon. It beats the hell out of flying coach."

Blaine laughs. "Well, considering our family has a private plane, that's not a big worry." As soon as the words leave his mouth, he realizes what he's done.

"You have a private plane?!" Amber practically screams. "Wow, so you can go to Paris for the weekend if you want. How did your family afford that? Kaitlyn, your parents aren't rich!"

Blaine doesn't say anything. He's pale as a ghost.

"It's only worth a hundred dollars," I say, covering fast. "But the sentimental value is huge."

"Huh?" Amber asks.

I stir my Coke with a straw, trying to look nonchalant. "Gordon's just messing with you. Our family does own a private plane. A private *model* plane. It's been passed down through generations. My great-great-grandfather got it at some special World

War II auction. It's kind of an inside joke."

Amber scrunches up her face. "That's weird."

"That's our family." Blaine looks relieved.

"Private plane," Scott laughs, slapping Blaine on the arm. "Dream big, buddy. Maybe someday it'll come true."

"Right you are," Blaine says, smiling.

I motion for Scott to let me out of the booth. "I'm going to wash my hands before the food gets here."

"Me too." Blaine slides out of the booth and I follow him over to the bathrooms. "Whew, that was a close call," he says. "Thanks for helping me out. You were awesome."

I glow at the unexpected compliment. "Back at ya."

Blaine walks into the men's restroom and I'm about to go into the women's when I hear someone call my name.

"Kaitlyn?" I turn around to find Morgan and Nathan standing next to the gumball machine.

"Hey, you guys!" I lean in to give her a hug and she pulls away.

Morgan stares at me, a hurt expression

clouding her face. "I can't believe you're here with Amber. When you told me you've been making lots of plans with your cousin, I didn't think that involved hanging out with the enemy."

I shift nervously from one foot to another. "It was sort of an accident."

"An accident? Oh, please. So this is why you didn't want to spend the night at my house last weekend. It had nothing to do with your dad making you stay home," she says. "You made that up because you'd rather hang out with *Amber*. Is she your new best friend?"

"Of course not!" I say hotly.

"And what about *him*?" She points toward our booth where Scott and Amber are sitting. "How'd you swing that? Did you sell your soul to Amber for a date with Scott Ryder?"

"No, it's not like that," I insist, but she cuts me off.

"Save it," she says, storming out the door.

We never make it back to the arcade. I'm not feeling much like playing air hockey, so Scott drops us off at my house after lunch.

"I had a stellar time," Amber says, hopping out of the car and giving Blaine a good-bye hug. "Call me. 'Kay?"

"Okay," Blaine says.

"I was thinking maybe you and I . . ." Amber begins. I trudge up the front steps and into the house. I don't want to hear the rest of her sentence. I don't want to stand by and watch her throw herself at Blaine anymore. It's been a crappy afternoon and I feel like being alone. I debate calling Morgan, but she's probably still out with Nathan. Besides, she probably wouldn't talk to me if I did call.

I do my algebra homework and then read the next chapter in my history book. Neither of these does much to lift my mood. I'm bummed about Amber and Blaine, and I feel awful about my fight with Morgan.

The only bright side of the day has been Scott Ryder. He actually gave me a hug when he dropped us off. Other than that, I'm feeling downright depressed.

Plus, I've been majorly slacking on my spy training. Oh, sure, I handled the private plane snafu pretty well, but that doesn't mean I'll be prepared next time.

I have to start taking this spy thing

more seriously and I have to start now. I shut my history book, put Morgan's *Alias* DVD in the machine, and hit play. Given the situation, it seems like the only appropriate thing to do.

Fifteen

I am so *not* Sydney Bristow. I could not even pass as Sydney Bristow's teenage sister. I am, at best, that nerdy, clumsy Marshall guy who rigs up all the computer gadgets and spy gear for Sydney and her spy pals.

This is a depressing thing to find out about yourself.

Sydney and I could not be more different if we tried. Consider the evidence: Sydney knows at least a hundred freakishly complex foreign languages. Whether traveling to the Ukraine or Uzbekistan, she's conversing like a pro. I, meanwhile, got a C plus on my last French test. *Not good.* And why did I sign up for a boring old language like French in the first place? Why didn't I sign up for one of Cop-a-Feel High's more exotic offerings, like Russian or Chinese?

Further proof that I am no Sydney: I am the world's biggest klutz. I can barely walk five feet without tripping. There's no way I could rappel down the side of some eighty-story building on a wire, or jump out of a plane and tackle a bad guy. And Sydney is always defusing some nuclear bomb—hello, I suck at chemistry. Not to mention the way she's always kicking some guy's ass beneath the strobe lights of a dance club. I'm not even old enough to get into dance clubs. I suppose I could weasel a fake ID, like the one Blaine has, but no one would believe it. I'm so short and scrawny I can barely pass for sixteen—which is my actual age. There's no way anyone would believe I was twenty-one. Amber Hamilton, maybe, but not me.

Come to think of it, Amber would make a terrific secret agent. She's sly, she's a great liar, she's a primo athlete, and she's got killer good looks. Great, just great. As if I needed one more reason to feel inferior to Amber. Now not only am I jealous of her awesome body and her supreme confidence, I'm green with jealousy over her super spy potential, too.

Things only get worse the next morning before school. It's pouring rain outside, so Mom drops us off on her way into work. This means we get there twenty minutes early. Usually, I like getting there early because it gives me time to catch up with Morgan before homeroom. But since our fight at Pike's Pizza yesterday, I don't know where things stand.

I catch sight of Morgan as soon as Blaine and I get out of the car. She's standing by herself under the awning over the front door, playing with her cell phone. I give her a tentative wave as we approach. She waves back. I turn to Blaine. "I'm going to go talk . . ."

I don't get a chance to finish my sentence. "I'll give you some privacy," Blaine says, heading into the school.

"Hey," I say, sidling up to Morgan.

"Hi." She tucks her cell phone in her pocket.

We stand there in silence for a minute, and then I take the plunge. "Look, I'm really sorry about what happened at Pike's. I never meant to hurt your feelings. Gordon and I were supposed to go to the arcade for a little while, and then Amber strong-armed her way into our afternoon. It definitely wasn't planned. I would never, ever, *ever* ditch you for Amber Hamilton. She sucks big time. She's not my best friend— she's not even a friend at all."

"I'm sorry, too." Morgan gives me a crooked smile. "I know you better than that. I was PMSing big time and I kinda overreacted." We share a brief hug. "So what was it like being on a date with Scott Ryder?" she squeals.

Suddenly, I feel shy. "Well, it wasn't exactly a date."

"It sure looked like one," she says, grinning. "Go you!"

"It was pretty exciting." I fill her in on all the details and Morgan listens intently. It's so great having my best friend back. Even though our fight was brief, it felt awful.

I lean over and give her an impromptu hug. "I've missed you."

"I've missed you, too."

"Yay, you made up!" Blaine says, coming up behind us. He's holding a small plastic baggie with a Pop Tart inside.

"Hey, where'd you get that?" I ask. Last time I checked we didn't have any Pop Tarts at my house.

"I found it," Blaine says. "It was in my locker, along with a note that said, 'Eat me.'"

He opens it up and prepares to take a bite. I feel a rush of panic coming over me. If there's one thing I've learned from all my spy training, it's that you don't eat suspicious food! It could be poisoned. "Blaine, no!" I shriek, grabbing hold of his arm. I pull as hard as I can, trying to fling the Pop Tart out of his hands. I yank with such force that Blaine goes toppling over. He stumbles forward a few feet, trying to regain his balance, and steps into the faculty parking lot, his body inches away from a moving car.

The driver honks the horn and Blaine leaps backward into the safety of the front lawn. He quickly rejoins Morgan and me under the awning, but it's too late. He's soaking wet. The Pop Tart lies crumbled on the ground. Thank God for small favors.

"What was that?" Morgan asks, her eyes wide. "You practically threw him in front of a moving car!"

"I was trying to, um, help," I try to explain.

Blaine is staring at me with a horrified expression on his face, but he doesn't say anything.

"Yikes, don't ever try to help me," Morgan says, shaking her head in disbelief. "You might get me killed."

"I wanted to protect Gordon," I say defensively. "It's not a good idea to eat suspicious food."

"Suspicious food?" Morgan asks. "It was a Pop Tart. There's no nutritional value, but other than that it's pretty harmless."

"We don't know who left it. It could be some kind of prank. Remember when you drank Gatorade spiked with Ex-Lax?"

It's a good save. Now Morgan takes my side.

"You're right," she says, the light bulb going off in her head. "Don't eat weird stuff," she lectures Blaine. "You never know who's tampered with it."

"I know who left it," Blaine says, regaining his composure. "It was Amber."

"Yuck." Morgan groans. "In that case, don't touch it with a ten-foot pole. Amber once spiked my Gatorade with *pooping pills*," she tells Blaine. "That girl is evil."

Blaine's not convinced. "Amber's a really sweet girl," he says. "I seriously doubt she would do something like that."

Before I can object, the first bell rings,

so we head into the school. I'm kind of glad for the distraction. Blaine seems pretty sold on Amber and I don't know if I want to bad-mouth her anymore. It's just not my style. Blaine goes upstairs to his homeroom and Morgan and I head toward our lockers.

"Kaitlyn, I have to be honest here. There's something I don't get," Morgan says, eyeing me suspiciously. "Right before you pushed *Gordon* into the parking lot, you did something really weird."

My pulse quickens. "I did?"

"Yeah." She stops in her tracks and looks me dead in the eyes. "You called him Blaine."

Sixteen

Oh. My. God. I've done it now. No amount of *Alias* watching or *Spy Manual* reading can make up for this blunder. Morgan's not clueless. There's no way she'll believe a stupid lie. But I have no choice. I have to cover. "No, I didn't. I said 'rain.'"

"It sounded an awful lot like Blaine to me."

I'm trapped. I'm backed against the wall. So I come clean with her. Sort of. "Okay, I did say Blaine. It's Gordon's nickname from when he was young. I try to never call him that, but it's a hard habit to break. And he *hates* it."

Morgan looks confused. "Why? It's not like it's some embarrassing nickname like Poopy Pants."

"Poopy Pants!" I burst out in nervous laughter.

"That's what we used to call my little cousin," she explains, popping a piece of gum in her mouth. "But Blaine is kind of a cool nickname. Unique. Where did he get it?"

I struggle to come up with something. Students are starting to pour into the building and the hallway is getting really crowded. I don't want anyone to overhear this story. "Uh, it's after David Blaine, the magician. Gordon used to be really into magic when he was growing up. He had this little top hat that he pulled a stuffed bunny out of and everything. He's way embarrassed so please, please, *please* don't bring it up to him. And please don't tell a soul," I plead with her. "Not Nathan, not the other soccer girls. No one. I'll get in so much trouble if you do."

"Okay, Nichols, I won't say anything." She offers me a piece of gum and I accept.

"Seriously. My life depends on it. I will get in huge trouble if my dad finds out I've told anyone." At least this part is true.

Something registers in Morgan's eyes.

"Wow, you are serious. But no need to freak. Your secret's safe with me." She smiles. "That's what best friends are for."

Morgan's mother gives us a ride home after school, and we stop by McDonald's first for something to eat. I'm snacking on Chicken McNuggets when Morgan's mom says, "You look very familiar, Gordon. Have we met before?"

Okay, this can't be good.

"I don't see how. This is my first time in St. Louis."

She thinks it over. "Have you ever been to Texas?"

I nearly throw up.

"I used to travel there all the time on business. I thought maybe we'd run into each other there," she continues.

Mrs. Riddick is a pharmaceutical sales rep. Before she and Morgan's dad divorced, she was on the road all the time.

"I'm from Georgia," Blaine says, taking a bite of his Big Mac. "Never been to Texas before."

"Hmm." Morgan's mom chomps on a fry. "I wonder where I've seen you then."

I rack my brain. What would Matt

Damon or Sydney Bristow do in a situation like this? "He kind of looks like that actor," I supply, trying to sound casual. Beneath the table my legs are shaking so badly that my knees are literally knocking together.

"Oh, yeah!" Morgan chimes in. "Gordon looks like Orlando Bloom, big time."

Mrs. Riddick snaps her fingers. "You're right! Orlando Bloom from *Pirates of the Caribbean*! That must be why you look so familiar. I bet you've heard that before."

"Once or twice," he says, ducking his head and taking another bite of food. He looks terribly uncomfortable.

I change the subject. "So do you know what's wrong with Mr. Clemmons?" I ask Morgan.

"I heard his appendix ruptured over the weekend."

Blaine looks alarmed. "Who's Mr. Clemmons?"

"The tenth-grade English teacher," I say. "He also happens to be my homeroom teacher. He's the one who gave me detention. He's not a very nice guy. But now it looks like we're going to have a substitute for the next couple of weeks, which sucks even worse."

Blaine munches on a fry. "I thought substitute teachers were supposed to be fun? Back home in Georgia," he says, careful not to slip up, "we always loved when our teacher was out sick. It meant we got to goof off all period."

"Normally it does. But this sub is a jerk."

"Mr. Dimitri," Morgan says, sticking out her tongue. "He seems like a real tool. Strict and boring. He yelled at two people at the beginning of first period because they hadn't finished reading *Macbeth*." Morgan's section is on a different book than mine. "Then when we were discussing the play, it turned out Mr. Dimitri didn't have a clue what he was talking about. How can he get mad at his students when he hasn't even read the work himself? He's the worst teacher ever." She swipes one of my McNuggets.

"I can't believe this, but I actually miss Mr. Clemmons," I say. "I would definitely rather have him over this Dimitri creep."

"Hopefully Mr. Clemmons will be back soon," Mrs. Riddick says. She polishes off the rest of her burger. "Are you guys almost ready to go?"

"Definitely," I say, tossing my empty McNugget container into the trash. I'm ready to get out of there before Morgan's mom can ask any more questions.

"We had a close call today," Blaine tells my dad over dinner later that night. He recounts the conversation with Morgan's mom.

"I was afraid of something like this," Dad says, setting down his knife and fork. "That's part of why we brought you to St. Louis. You got some exposure in the papers back in Texas, but you haven't been profiled nationally."

"You've been in the newspaper?" I ask Blaine, between bites of chicken casserole.

"Mmm-hmm. There have been tons of articles about my father, and sometimes they mention me."

Dad massages his temple. He looks tired, worried. "Do you think Mrs. Riddick believed your story?"

Blaine chews on his lower lip. "I hope so. I can't be sure."

"Gordon handled it like a pro," I tell Dad. "Morgan's mom completely bought it."

"Kaitlyn's the pro," he says, returning

the compliment. "My mind went blank but she came up with a lie straight away."

Dad looks impressed. "Good job," he says approvingly.

"We're celebrating our daughter being a good liar," Mom says, dabbing at the corners of her mouth with a napkin. "I never thought this day would come."

"It's for a good cause," Dad says. "Now, I do have some news. Thing are going very smoothly with the business deal. It's moving even quicker than we'd hoped. Everything should be completed within the next month or two. Hopefully, we'll catch the perps before then. But even if we don't, once the deal is signed, sealed, and delivered, Gordon can return home. With any luck, we'll have you back in time for your junior prom. Hope you've got a date in mind," Dad cracks, looking very proud of himself.

But I feel miserable. Blaine's barely been here two weeks, and already the thought of seeing him go completely depresses me.

Seventeen

"Brace yourself," Morgan says, catching me before homeroom the following morning. "This is bad."

"What's bad?" I ask nervously.

"Amber. At least I think it's Amber. She's . . . well. See for yourself." Morgan whips out her cell. "This picture was e-mailed to everyone on the girls' soccer team this morning," she says, handing me the phone. "Try not to freak out, Nichols. I know it seems bad, but . . . you'll be okay. I swear. If I survived crapping my pants on the soccer field, then you can survive this."

Despite Morgan's warning, nothing can prepare me for the image on the screen. As

I stare at the cell phone I feel frozen, sick to my stomach. It's me—only I'm half naked. It's a picture of me changing for gym class. I'm standing there without my shirt, my tiny, nonexistent breasts displayed in all their flat-chested glory. Thank God I'm wearing a bra. Amber's best friend Kayla is in my gym class. She must have snapped the photo when I wasn't paying attention.

I stand there, too numb to move or even speak. And then, finally, the words come. "Noooooooooo!" I cry. I start whimpering, making horrible, guttural sounds. Morgan grabs hold of me, steadying me in her arms. "It's okay. It just went out to the girls' soccer team. At least no guys have seen it."

As if on cue, one of the football jocks comes sailing by. "Hey, look, it's Nudie Nichols!" he says, gesturing at me. "Show us a little skin, eh?"

"Oh, God," I say, running around the side of the school. And there, behind one of the large dumpsters, I break down in tears.

It's worse than I ever could have imagined. The photo has spread like wildfire—forwarded to cell phones all over school.

I go through the rest of the day being

called Nudie Nichols. In every class I can hear kids snickering behind my back. I can feel their eyes boring into the back of my head. In the halls people laugh and point as I walk by. It's awful. By lunchtime I'm so upset I hide out in one of the bathroom stalls. Morgan tracks me down there.

"It's no use, I'm not coming out," I tell her as she bangs on the door.

"I have something that will make you feel better."

"*Nothing* can make me feel better."

She laughs a wicked, maniacal laugh. "How about a little revenge?"

"I don't know. . . ." I'm reluctant. I'm too humiliated and depressed to think about anything but my own pain.

"So, I've been thinking," Morgan tells me. "All this time we've let Amber pick on us, walk all over us. And we've done nothing to stop her; we're easy targets. Maybe if we stand up for ourselves, if we fight fire with fire, then she'll back off and leave us alone—for good."

Well . . . there could be something to what Morgan's saying. I crack open the door. "What did you have in mind?"

Morgan rubs her hands together in

anticipation. "I think I've found *the* perfect thing." She reaches into her backpack and retrieves a stack of magazines. "Ta da!" she announces. "I swiped these from the school library after first period."

I wipe my tearstained face, then stare at the magazines in confusion. "What are we going to do, fill out, like, fifty subscription cards in Amber's name?"

"Hmm, that's not bad," Morgan muses, leaning against the stall door. "But I was going for something more immediate. I wanna be there to see her reaction." She rapidly thumbs through the pages, then comes to a sudden stop. "Here it is!" She passes the magazine to me.

I stare down and see a full-page tampon ad, complete with the words "New anti-leak system for your heaviest days."

"Ew, gross!"

"Don't you get it?" Morgan asks, waving the ad in my face. "These magazines have like ten billion tampon ads in each one." She flips through another magazine and stops at a tampon ad, proving her point. "We're going to tear out a dozen or so of these and put them on everything Amber touches. Her desk, her locker, her soccer basket in the girls' changing room. We'll blanket her with tampon ads!"

It's pretty mean—not the sort of thing I would ordinarily do—but I'm feeling desperate. And giving Amber a taste of her own medicine might take the edge off my own crushing embarrassment. "So when should we do it?"

"Right now! Everyone's in the cafeteria so it's the perfect time to plaster her locker. And then you can get to English class early and leave a couple on her desk!"

"You really think this is a good idea?" I ask. As much as I hate Amber, I can't help feeling a lump in the pit of my stomach that tells me this is going to be bad.

Morgan nods her head. "We have to do it. She's got it coming."

I still feel a little funny about it, but I push those thoughts aside and set to work clipping out tampon ads. Having something to do distracts me from imagining hordes of people looking at the picture of me in my bra.

Once we've got a decent-size stack, we put phase one of the plan into action. Morgan and I duck into the main office and sneak a small tape dispenser when the secretary, Mrs. Millikan, isn't looking. Then we get down to business. We take turns decorating and standing guard. We have to work quickly. Lunch period is almost over and we don't want anyone to catch us. In no time flat, we've covered Amber's locker with a collage of tampon photos. In the middle is the *piéce de resistance*: a huge colorful headline that says BLOATING, GAS, CONSTIPATION. Beneath it are the words "Is stress taking its toll on your tummy?" We ditched that part, though; it was funnier with just the three big words. After we've finished with the locker we go our separate ways, with Morgan heading toward the sports locker room and me taking off for Mr. Dimitri's English class.

I'm the first one there. I can't believe how perfectly we've timed this! I only have one tampon ad left, but it's a goody. It has an enormous photo of a tampon on it, along with the words "Your monthly friend." After a few seconds of debate, I decide to tape the ad to the back of Amber's chair. I figure that's the safest. Hopefully she'll sit down without even noticing it. Wouldn't that be a riot? I would pee my pants laughing if Amber sits through English class with a giant tampon photo attached to the back of her chair.

As soon as I'm finished taping it up, I dart out of the classroom and make my way down the hall. The last thing I want to do is be caught red-handed. I wander back into the office and replace the tape dispenser on the front counter. Thankfully, Mrs. Millikan is, like, the least observant person on the planet. She's always too busy reading cheesy paperback romance novels to notice what the students are doing.

I casually stroll out of the office and over to the girls' bathroom. I have a few minutes to kill before I need to get to English class. I want to make sure I get there after some other students have arrived (but before the late bell—the last thing I need is another tardy). That way, no one will consider me a suspect. I stop in front of the bathroom mirror and reapply my makeup. I dig into my purse and locate my container of loose powder. Then I spend several minutes applying a fresh coat of eye shadow and mascara. I smooth down my hair, minimizing the frizziness as much as possible. I spend so much time in front of the bathroom mirror that I'm almost late for class. But I can't help it. Amber Hamilton is about to be taken down a couple of notches and I want to look my absolute best for it.

Eighteen

Amber is already sitting down, thumbing through her English folder, when I get to class. She looks up when I walk through the door.

"Damn!" I mutter under my breath. I can't believe she's already here! Amber never gets to class early.

I wanted to be there to watch her freak out over the tampon ad, but I've screwed around for too long and I've missed it. My eyes dart over and I see that the ad is gone. She must have seen it right away and taken it down. That sucks. Oh well, at least we still have the locker prank.

"Hi freak," she says, giving me a nasty smile as I make my way to my desk. "You know something, Nudie Nichols? Your skin has been downright awful lately. Looks like somebody could use some Accutane," she announces loudly.

I turn bright red, but I don't say anything back. It's like my mom is always telling me: It's best to ignore people like Amber. (Of course, the fact that I've stuck a tampon ad on her desk isn't exactly ignoring her. But whatever.)

I don't think about Amber much more during class. We're reading *Beowulf*, which I find utterly boring. Mr. Dimitri makes it ten times worse by talking in this monotone, nasal voice. I'm barely able to stay awake during class and take down notes. The hour goes by at a snail's pace while Mr. Dimitri drones on and on about the symbolism and how the monster represents all these important things. Painful stuff, indeed. Mr. Clemmons had better hurry up and get well. His class may not be lively, but it's not downright torturous.

When the bell rings I throw my books in my backpack and stand to leave. It's then that I see it.

Standing a few feet in front of me is Amber Hamilton. She's running her fingers through her long red hair, fluffing it out like she always does. But I barely notice this. What catches my attention is her butt. More specifically, what's on her butt. The tampon ad has somehow gotten attached to the seat of her pants, kind of like a KICK ME sign, only lower down. And lightyears more embarrassing.

It's all I can do to keep from laughing as I follow Amber out into the hall. I see two guys jab each other in the side and point at Amber's butt. "Amber, did you have a little accident?" one of them cackles. "Nasty, nasty!" the other says. They're so busy laughing at Amber they don't even notice Nudie Nichols, a.k.a. me. They run over and tell a few of the jocks who are hanging out by the lockers. One of them puts his fingers in his mouth and whistles. Amber turns around and blows him a kiss, and he doubles over with laughter.

She looks confused, mortified. Suddenly, I feel bad. *Really* bad. I never meant for Amber to actually *wear* the tampon ad. Maybe we've gone too far. Just because she's a nasty wench doesn't mean we have to stoop to her level. No one should have to suffer the way I have today—not even Amber Hamilton.

I rush to catch up with her, but Amber's too far ahead of me and she's moving too fast. People keep darting out and blocking my way. Before I know it, she's rounded the corner and disappeared out of sight.

I shake it off. *Amber deserves this*, I remind myself, as I hurry down the hall to my next class.

The rest of the day goes by in a blur. Part of me feels way guilty about what we did to Amber. But another, meaner part of me is glad she finally got what she deserved.

I meet with a few of the newspaper reporters after school to go over future story assignments. I'm kind of hoping Scott will be there, but he's off covering a basketball game.

Once I'm finished, I pick up my bag and walk out into the hall. I'm just passing the girls' bathroom when I feel a hand reach out and grab me.

"Kaitlyn Nichols, just who I wanted to see!" My pulse quickens. It's Amber Hamilton. And she looks *furious*. She guides me into the bathroom, where Erica Lewis and Kayla Hollinger, two of her best friends, are waiting.

"Uh, hi," I mumble, swallowing hard.

Why oh why did I have to go to the news-room today? Why couldn't I have snuck out with the rest of the students an hour ago?

"Hi yourself," Kayla says. "We know what you did."

I feign innocence. "What are you talking about?"

"Don't play dumb!" Kayla hisses.

"Oh, she's not playing." Amber cackles. "Kaitlyn really is stupid. How else can you explain her actions?"

"Guys, I don't know what you think I did, but—"

"Shove it," Erica says. "My boyfriend Marcus saw you tape that tampon ad to Amber's butt."

"I didn't tape it to her butt!" I exclaim. And then I realize what I've done. I want to kick myself. They've got me. There's nothing to do now but come clean. "Okay, so I did do it. But it was her desk, not her butt."

"Marcus said it was her butt," Erica insists. "And he wouldn't lie."

"Unlike you," Kayla tells me. "You're nothing but a jealous, lying little brat. But you know what? You'll get yours. When you screw with Amber, you screw with all of us."

"That's right," Erica agrees.

I'm not sure what I expected to happen, but this is not going well. "Look . . . I . . . I'm sorry. We were angry, Morgan and me. You guys have done a lot of shitty stuff to us. The Ex-Lax incident, and just today the picture of me changing for gym class."

Erica laughs. "Yeah, that was one of our best tricks yet!" She, Amber, and Kayla exchange high fives.

"What can I say, Nudie? You and your dorky little friend Morgan make such great targets," Amber says.

Kayla giggles. "Get out of here." She gives me a tiny push toward the door.

"Not so fast," Amber says, blocking my exit. She moves forward until she's so close we're practically touching. "You realize what this means, scrub."

I shrug. I'm starting to get annoyed. So what if they're a bunch of bullies? So what if they're ten times more popular than I am? I don't have to lie down and take this. It's time to fight back.

"We're at war," Amber says, her face a few inches from mine.

I snort. "Ooh, I'm really scared."

"You should be," Kayla warns.

"Well, I'm not. Whatever you're planning, go ahead. Bring it," I say, keeping my voice hollow and emotionless. "I can handle anything." I think I've stunned them. They didn't expect me to stand up for myself and they're momentarily speechless. I walk out of the bathroom and head off down the hall.

As I'm rounding the corner to leave the building I run into Blaine. He has a strange look on his face. "Did you . . . did you do it?" he asks as I approach.

"Do what?" I feel my pulse quicken.

"To Amber. Did you put those ads everywhere? Because that's a terrible thing to do to someone. I wouldn't think you'd stoop to that level, but I keep hearing rumors."

"Gordon, I—I had to. I had to get back at her for what she did."

Blaine shakes his head. "You didn't *have* to do anything," he says. "You *chose* to. I know you've had a rough day. I heard about the picture," he says, and my face flushes. "But you don't even know if Amber had anything to do with that. She might be totally innocent. But you jumped the gun and attacked her." He looks in my eyes for a long time. "I never thought you were that kind of person, Kaitlyn. I guess I was wrong."

He walks out the door before I can say anything else. I stand there, horrified.

What have I done?

"Mom, can I talk to you about something?" I ask, poking my head in my parents' bedroom.

My mother looks up from her laptop. "Of course, honey. What's on your mind?"

It's later that night and I'm feeling really bummed about Blaine. He's not talking to me. He's right, I did make a choice. But it's so frustrating, because if he only knew what kind of girl she was . . . if he could only see how vile she is, and how much she humiliated me today, then maybe he'd understand.

But I guess my job isn't to *make* him see anything. I have to let him live his own life, find out for himself. I can try to protect him, but I can't control him.

I've decided to confide in my mother. That's kind of a weird thing to do, right? I mean, who willingly talks to their *mother* about their guy problems? But with Blaine it's different. I can't call Morgan and spill, the way I usually do. She'd be thoroughly grossed out if I suddenly called and confessed I was having feelings for my "cousin."

"This thing with Blaine—"

She shakes her head. "Gordon."

"Oh, right. Sorry. This thing with *Gordon* is a little awkward for me."

"I thought it might be." Mom motions for me to sit down on her bed. "Go on."

I sit down next to her. "Well, ever since Gordon moved in here it feels like everything's changed. Amber Hamilton, who is my sworn enemy, suddenly started falling all over herself to be my friend. Morgan and I drifted apart, although now we're back together. Nothing makes sense anymore."

"Oh, honey." She pats my arm.

"And Gordon! I have no idea what's up with him. Sometimes we get along great, and other times I think he thinks I'm just some stupid little kid. It's so confusing."

My mom smiles at me. "You like him, don't you?"

Without meaning to, I nod. Now that the cat's out of the bag, I might as well be one hundred percent honest. "Gordon's majorly out of my league and would never like me back in ten million years. And even if he did, we couldn't be together because he's going back to Texas and I'm staying here. Once he leaves we'll probably never see each other again. I just don't know what to do, Mom." I burst into tears. "And now he's not even speaking to me!" I wail.

"He's not speaking to you?" she asks, puzzled. "I noticed he seemed distant today, but I wasn't sure what that was all about.

"I did something kind of bad to somebody, and Gordon found out and now he's lost all respect for me." I try hard to control my tears, but they start falling faster. Through a series of sniffles and gulps, I fill her in on the whole sordid story—I tweak it a little, leaving out key elements of the tampon incident and the Nudie Nichols picture. I can't tell Mom *everything*.

When I'm finished with the story, Mom sets down her laptop and comes over to give me a hug. "Oh, Kaitlyn, I was afraid of this happening. As soon as your dad brought Gordon here, I saw how well you two were getting along. It was only natural."

"I just wish I didn't feel this way," I sob. "I just wish everything could go back to being normal."

"It will. You'll see. These things have a

funny way of working themselves out." She hugs me tighter. "And for what it's worth, I don't think Gordon will stay mad at you for long. You have to realize that he's going through a lot too—being separated from his family and friends. I know he appreciates everything you've done to make him feel at home. In fact, if I had to bet on it, I'd say he likes you, too."

I'm taken aback. "What?" And then I realize. "You're my mother. You have to say things like that."

"I'm also a relationship columnist," she says. "And I'm giving you my completely professional, nonmotherly opinion. I see the way Gordon looks at you. I see the way his face lights up when you're in the room. He likes you, too."

I blink back tears. "Really?"

"Really. You two seem to have made a great connection."

"Wow." I let out a huge sigh. "That makes me feel a little better. Like maybe I'm not crazy, after all."

"You're not crazy," Mom says, stroking my hair. "But there's something else, Kaitlyn." Her face falls. "It's sweet that you two have become so close, but you have to be realistic about things. Pretty soon Gordon will leave. He'll go back home and I don't know when, or if, you'll get to see him again. I want you to be prepared for that."

At her words, a fresh set of tears tumbles down my cheeks. "But I thought you said he liked me. I thought you said we had a great connection."

"You do." My mom sighs sadly. "But great connection or not, some things just aren't meant to be."

We talk for a while longer, and I promise Mom that I'll put my feelings for Blaine aside. It kills me to do it. The last thing I want is for Blaine to go out with skanky Amber Hamilton. But I don't see what choice I have. If I follow my heart, I risk his safety. It's quite a predicament.

Matt Damon never faced anything like this in *The Bourne Identity*. Ditto James Bond.

Nineteen

"Are you sitting down?" Morgan screams. "I have amazing news for you!"

It's the following night and I'm moping around my room. I'm still feeling awful about Blaine. He seems so disappointed in me. In fact, he's been going out of his way to avoid me. He didn't walk with me to school; he got a ride from Amber's mom instead. And after class he hung around in the library until my mom could pick him up.

It's depressing that he doesn't want to be around me. I don't know what to do to win back his trust.

"All right, I'm sitting down now." I flop back on my bed.

"You're gonna freak out when you hear this!"

"Freak out good or freak out bad?"

"FREAK OUT GOOD!" Morgan yells.

I hold the phone away from my ear. "Geez, can you keep it down? I have a headache." I'm not trying to be grumpy. But I feel so bummed out.

"Your headache is about to magically disappear when I tell you this. Guess what?"

"What?" I play along.

"Scott Ryder likes you!"

"Shut up," I groan. But, secretly, I'm intrigued. "Why do you think he likes me? I already told you that day at Pike's wasn't a date."

"Maybe not. But I bet Scott wishes it was!"

I sigh. As much as I want to believe it's true, I just can't. "Morgan, where are you getting all this?"

"A-hem," she clears her throat. "Go to MySpace."

I move over to my computer and type the website into my browser. "Okay, what am I looking for?"

"Scott's profile."

I log in and call up Scott's profile page.

And there, right smack dab at the top, is a picture of me.

"Oh my God!" I shriek, nearly dropping the phone. I'm in Scott Ryder's Top Eight! Not only that, but I'm number two! I've even displaced Amber! Out of all two hundred and sixty-seven people on Scott Ryder's MySpace Friends' list, I rate second.

It's thrilling, all right, but part of me still feels sad. Until I get things worked out with Blaine, I won't feel right.

Things continue to be awkward with Blaine, so I spend the next couple of days avoiding him altogether. Instead, I throw myself into my article for the *Courier*. Writing about plumbing is pretty much the dullest thing on the planet. Now I understand how Mom felt when she got saddled with all those craptastic assignments for the *St. Louis Observer*. No wonder she wanted to become a sex columnist.

I interview the assistant principal, the head of maintenance, and a few of the teachers who use that bathroom a lot. Everyone is really nice and forthcoming—with one exception. The creepy substitute teacher, Mr. Dimitri, bites my head off when I try to talk to him.

"I know you want to be a hotshot journalist like your mother, but I don't have time for this," he says, literally shutting his classroom door in my face. Jerk! Mr. Clemmons would never do a thing like that. I swear, Mr. Dimitri is the worst teacher I've ever had. He's mean, arrogant, and he doesn't even seem to know the material.

I finally finish my article and turn it in to our managing editor, Miller, before school on Thursday. I've just left the *Courier* newsroom when I run into Scott.

"Hey!" he says, giving me a high five. He holds my hand for a second and squeezes it. "Did you hear the good news?"

"What good news?"

"Your cousin's got a date with Amber," Scott says.

My jaw drops. "He does?"

"Yeah, they're going to the Valentine's dance." Scott grins from ear to ear.

It looks like Mom was wrong. Blaine and I don't have a connection after all. I shake the thought out of my head. It doesn't matter. I've got Scott. Wonderful, beautiful Scott Ryder. Scott Ryder who put *me* in his Top Eight on MySpace. Scott Ryder who hugged *me* the other day. I shouldn't even care about Blaine. . . .

"Give Gordon my congrats. A few weeks at Cop-a-Feel, and he's already dating Amber Hamilton. That's some accomplishment."

I stand there, dumbfounded.

"So I was thinking, this works out perfectly," Scott says, ignoring my pained expression. "Why don't you tell your parents you're staying at Amber's house the night of the dance. And then Amber can tell hers that she's staying with you."

"Huh?" I stare at him, confused. "Why would I need to do that?"

"That way you can spend the night at my house," he says, bumping his hip against mine. "You know, after the dance."

I stare at him. "Are you asking me to go to the dance with you?" I say at last.

"Well, duh," Scott replies, as if it were totally obvious.

"So your parents are out of town or something?" A horrible feeling washes over me.

"No, they'll be there. But they don't care what I do. We can have the whole downstairs to ourselves. And, of course, we'll have the privacy of my bedroom." He winks at me.

"Oh." I swallow hard. "I see."

"So, are you up for it?" He leans down and brushes his lips gently against mine. For a moment, I feel myself melt into his kiss. Then we pull apart, and he says, "Don't worry, Katie, I have thick walls."

"Thick walls," I repeat, unable to stomach where this conversation is going. *Please don't let him mean that. Please don't let things turn out this way.* I'm not sure how to respond. "I don't know, maybe."

Scott tips his head down and looks me in the eyes. "Come on, don't be a baby. Your cousin and Amber are totally up for that."

I feel sick. "They are?"

"Hell, yeah. All the guys score at the Valentine's dance. It's tradition."

I take a deep breath and finally my brain starts to kick in. I can't believe how wrong I was about this guy. "Scott, I'm sorry, but I'm just not up for that."

He shrugs. "Suit yourself. But you're missing out. *Big time.*"

"I think I'll manage," I tell him snidely.

Scott snickers. "I'm not the kind of guy to say 'I told you so,' which is why I'm going to get this out in the open right now. If you pass on this opportunity, Katie, you'll regret it."

Now I'm starting to get pissed off. "Excuse me?"

"I'm just sayin' that if you let me get away you'll live to regret it. Girls always do."

I can't believe how cocky he is! Why did I never notice this before? "Let you get away?" I demand, feeling my anger grow. "So, what, you're telling me if I don't spend the night at your house, then our date is off?"

He shakes his head. "Of course not. But I don't know if I'll be up for going out with you again. It will kind of be over before it starts."

"You know something," I say, fixing him with my best pissed-off glare, "I think it already is."

Maybe all the TV watching and spy training have paid off. Scott looks completely stunned, as though I've just zinged him with a Sydney Bristow–style kick.

It's a great line to exit on. So I push my way out of the newsroom and tear off down the hall.

"At least you found out what an ass he is now," Morgan says, when I catch up with her in the bathroom a few minutes later. Through tears I manage to tell her about my breakup with Scott. Can it even be called a breakup when we weren't officially going out?

"Maybe it's not what you think about Gordon. Maybe Amber bullied him into going," Morgan continues. "It's probably not a real date. They're probably just going as friends."

"Well, hello, girls," Amber says, coming into the bathroom. I swear to God, that girl has impeccable timing. She always knows exactly how to show up and make a bad situation worse.

"Big plans for the weekend?" she asks, taking out a tube of Lip Venom plumper from her purse. "Oh, wait, I forgot. You two wenches are dateless for the big dance tomorrow night. I heard you blew it with Scott."

I ignore her. I couldn't care less what she has to say.

Unfortunately, Morgan takes the bait.

"Not that it's any of your business, but we're choosing to go without dates."

This isn't exactly true. We're more dateless by default. Nathan is home sick with strep throat, and I've officially ditched Scott Ryder. There aren't a lot of options at this point.

"Just because you tricked Gordon into taking you is no reason to be so smug," Morgan rants. "He's probably regretting the second he said yes to you. If he weren't such a gentleman I bet he'd take it back."

Amber bursts out laughing, and then covers her mouth as if trying to hide it.

"What's so funny?" Morgan demands, squaring off against her.

"Nothing. It's just kind of humorous how clueless you two are. My God, Kaitlyn, Gordon is your cousin and you barely know him at all! You spend all this time trying to pal around with him. Yet everyone can see how much he can't stand you."

"Shut up, Hamilton," Morgan says, waving her hand dismissively. "What do you know?"

"I know plenty." Amber stands in front of the mirror, carefully applying Lip Venom to her already pouty mouth. "And trust me, Gordon can't stand either one of you."

"You're just jealous."

"Please. Of what? I have a date for the dance, unlike you two losers. You and Nathan are kaput," she says, pointing a finger at Morgan, "and Kaitlyn completely threw herself at Scott Ryder only to get a big fat rejection."

"I did not throw myself at him!" I say hotly. "*He* asked *me* to go to the dance and I called it off when I realized what his real intentions were."

"Sure, whatever you say." Amber purses her lips in front of the mirror. Thanks to the Lip Venom, her mouth is now reaching Angelina Jolie proportions. "This stuff tingles when you put it on. It's supposed to feel awesome when you kiss someone while you're wearing it. I guess I'll find out when I kiss Gordon at the dance. You know something?" she says, as she heads out the door. "I've never broken up a family before. Friendships, yes, boyfriends and girlfriends, yes. But a family? That's a new one. Should be fun."

For the rest of the week, all anyone can talk about is Blaine and Amber. Whenever a hot new couple debuts at school, they instantly become the center of attention. I try not to let the gossip get to me, but it's hard. I know the second I see Blaine and Amber together, I'm going to lose it. So the next day, when I catch sight of Blaine coming into the cafeteria during lunch, I bolt. I leave my half-eaten chicken sandwich sitting on the table and I run out into the hall.

"Kaitlyn, wait!" Blaine calls, coming up behind me.

I can't talk to him now—I'm not ready. I need some time to cool down. I take off running and don't stop until I've rounded the corner and ducked into the safety of the newsroom. The other staffers are at lunch, which is good since I don't feel like talking to anybody. I plop down in front of one of the computers and throw my head in my hands. I take a few deep breaths to steady my nerves. I don't know why I feel so emotional about all this. So what if Blaine goes out with Amber? It's not like I have any claim to him. It's not like he's my boyfriend. We've only known each other a couple of weeks. And I don't even have any reason to think that he likes me, except for what my mom said. And she's my mom! She thinks every teenage guy should see my inner beauty. So there's no reason for me to be upset about this. No reason at all.

"Penny for your thoughts."

"What?" I look up to find Blaine standing in front of me. I didn't even hear him come in.

"It's an expression my dad uses whenever he wants to know what's on my mind."

I stand up and turn toward the door. "I better be going. I have to get to class."

"Come on, don't give me that," Blaine says. "There's still twenty minutes left during lunch. Can we talk for a minute?" His voice is really soft all of a sudden.

"Yeah," I say, even though I don't feel like discussing this. "I thought you were mad at me."

He shakes his head. "I was. For a little while. But then I realized, after what you'd been through . . . everybody makes mistakes."

I shrug. "I didn't mean to go after Amber like that. Well, I guess I did. Look, I know she's your girlfriend now and all, but there's a lot of stuff you don't know about her. She's not a nice person, Bla—Gordon. I don't mean to bad-mouth her, but I feel like I have to warn you."

"My girlfriend?" he repeats, looking confused. "Man, things get twisted. There's a crazy rumor going around school that I am dating Amber Hamilton," Blaine says, brushing a lock of hair off his face. "That's what I came here to tell you. I'm not dating her."

"You're not?"

"She asked me to the dance yesterday morning—as friends. Nothing more. I thought it would be fun. But I don't want anything more with her."

"Well, what are you waiting for?" I snort. "Every guy in school would give his right arm for a date with Amber. Well, except the gay ones."

"What am I waiting for?" Blaine asks. "Your dad would say the same thing. He keeps encouraging me to 'blend in,' go on dates, be a normal teenager."

I sigh. "Yep, that's part of the plan."

"And I'm okay with that," Blaine says. He steps forward until he's right beside me. "But I don't want to date Amber."

My pulse starts to speed up. It's electrifying being this close to him. "You don't?"

"No." He looks me straight in the eyes. "I like someone else."

I can barely breathe. It's happening. It's

really happening. I can feel it—that unmistakable moment when you know someone is about to kiss you. He takes my hands and slowly pulls me to him.

"Kaitlyn," Blaine says, his voice slightly above a whisper. He cups my face in his hands and moves closer, until we're almost touching. Then he leans in slowly and his lips brush against mine. The kiss is soft and gentle, and it feels so good I think I might die. When he kisses me the whole world disappears. I can't hear the fluorescent lights buzzing overhead, or smell the chemicals coming from the newspaper darkroom. I'm not aware of anything but him.

Blaine kisses me for a minute and then he pulls away. He holds my hands in his, rubbing his fingers over my palm. "Did you feel . . . ?" he asks, his voice trailing off. "Was it . . . ?"

"Yeah." I nod. "*Amazing.*" I gaze at him for a moment. "I can't believe it. I thought you just saw me as an annoying little sister type who's always tripping over herself."

Blaine laughs. "Are you kidding? Kaitlyn, you are so funny and fun to be with. You're nothing like the other girls I know, who only care about my parents' money or the way I look. Being with you is so easy and natural. You're like a breath of fresh air."

"That's how I feel about you, too," I tell him.

Blaine lets out a big sigh and sinks back against the wall. "So what happens now?"

"I don't know."

We stare at each other.

"You'll be leaving soon," I say. I can sense a lump forming in my throat. This is not the conversation I want to be having right now. I just want to bask in the awesomeness of it all.

"I will."

"And we're supposedly, um, cousins." The second I say it I feel kind of sick. Why in the world did I bring *that* up? Am I trying to ruin the mood?

He drops my hands. "In other words, this isn't going to work."

"Blaine, I wish it could," I say. I have to choke the words out. "But I don't see how it possibly can. There are too many obstacles."

"Okay, then. That's what I needed to know." He looks hurt. "I'd better go." He turns and leaves. I follow him out the door.

"Bla—Gordon!" I say, catching myself just in time. "I'm sorry."

"Don't be," he calls over his shoulder, but keeps walking. I slump against the wall and bow my head.

"Nichols." I look up and find Morgan staring at me. I've never seen her so shocked. "I saw you."

Oh, no! Please, tell me this is a bad dream.

"I saw you *kissing* Gordon. Kissing your *cousin*," she says.

I chew on my lower lip. I have no answer for her. There's nothing I can possibly say.

"Hold on a second. He's . . . he's not your cousin, is he?" Morgan says, the realization dawning on her.

I don't respond. I can't. My head is spinning and my lips are still tingling from the kiss. And I'm scared. Terrified.

"What's going on?" Morgan asks, her hands on her hips. "'Cause you sure haven't been telling me the truth."

"I'll tell you everything later," I swear. "As soon as I can."

"Why are you being so secretive?"

"It's so complicated," I say. I need to sit down. My knees are weak. I try to focus on the situation at hand. We've been busted. There's no way I can continue lying to Morgan. But I can't tell her here. It's too risky. "Please, just give me some time," I say. "I can't say anything right now, but I'll tell you everything soon. It will all make sense, I swear."

She looks worried. "Whoa . . . you're serious."

I nod. "I swear to God, Morgan, I would do it now if I could. It'll all be clear soon. But for the moment, please don't tell anyone what you saw," I whisper. "If you do, it could endanger Gordon's life."

"Don't worry," Morgan says, making a zipping motion across her mouth. "My lips are sealed."

I give her a quick hug. "Thanks, you're the best."

Dad is waiting for me when I get home from school. I'm surprised to see him. He usually doesn't get off work until later in the day. He's decked out in a ridiculous pastel green jogging suit with purple stripes down the side. He's obviously been home for a while. Dad wouldn't be caught dead wearing something like this to the office.

Now that I think about it, he's been coming home early a lot lately. I guess they're cutting him some slack since, technically, he's brought his work home with him. Protecting Blaine is a twenty-four-hour-a-day job.

"Kaitlyn, can I talk to you for a minute?" he asks when I come in the front door. He motions for me to follow him.

"Yeah, no prob." I trail after Dad into the living room.

He brushes a stack of condoms aside—props for Mom's column—and sits down at the desk. "I know this is personal, but we really need to talk."

Uh-oh. This can't be good. Maybe he somehow found out about the kiss and he knows Blaine's cover is blown!

"Gordon told me Amber asked him to the Valentine's Day dance," Dad continues. "He also told me about the situation between you two."

I gulp. "He did?"

"Yes. And I know this is hard for you, Kaitlyn, but you have to distance yourself from Gordon. You can't get personally attached. And you certainly can't date him. That would never work with Gordon's cover. And, unfortunately, his cover takes precedence over everything else. You have to put his safety first."

I sink down on the couch. "But how am I supposed to distance myself? It's a little tricky considering he's living here."

Dad shakes his head. "I don't mean physically. I mean emotionally. That's one of the first things they teach you in the FBI. Never get emotionally involved in your cases. It will lead to failure every time."

I pick a piece of lint off my skirt. "It will?"

"Yes, it will. Every single time."

It's ironic, really. I spent all this time preparing for my new undercover life. I watched films, I studied the *Ultimate Spy Manual*. But I broke the number one rule of being a secret agent. I got emotionally involved.

Twenty

There is something totally depressing about school dances. There's no getting around it. No matter how carefully you plan or how awesome you expect things to turn out, it always winds up being a huge letdown.

This time is different, though. Unlike the last school dance I attended—the one where Jared spent the entire night smoking cigarettes outside with his slacker friends while I stood in a corner by myself—I am prepared for the worst. I have low expectations going in. At least that way I won't be disappointed. In some ways I'm glad I'm going without a date. I'm so fed up with guys at the moment that I'm thinking about swearing off them for the rest of the school year.

Blaine carpools with Amber, Kayla, and Scott the Jerk. My dad drops Morgan and me off in front of the gym around seven. "I'll be back at eleven to get you girls," he says, waving as we get out of the car. "Have fun!"

I step out of the car. "Bye, Dad."

Morgan eyes me sympathetically. "Are you sure you're up for this? You seem really upset about this whole thing with Amber and . . ." Her voice trails off. "I'm not sure what to call him."

"Gordon is best," I say, making my way across the parking lot. "I'm sorry I can't tell you everything now," I say in a voice barely above a whisper.

"It's okay." Morgan pats me on the arm. "You can fill me in when you're ready. Now, are you sure you're in the mood to go to this crappy dance? 'Cause we can go back home if you want. I'm totally up for a night of movies and pizza if that's what you're craving."

"Thanks." I smile. "But I'll be all right. This whole thing just feels so craptastic."

"Been there, my friend."

We walk into the gym and get drinks from the concession stand. Then we make our way over to a far wall where we can observe the action. There isn't much going on. Blaine and Amber are dancing to a fast song out in the middle of the floor, and it feels like all eyes are on them. As they sail by, Blaine holds up his hand and waves slightly. I smile back at him.

"God, you would think Mr. Dimitri would lighten up," Morgan says, nudging me. "He looks like he's freaking constipated or something."

I follow her gaze. The substitute teacher is standing in the corner of the room, a look of psychotic concentration on his face.

"Some people should not be teachers," Morgan says. "That guy's been nothing but one giant ass ever since he got here."

Casey from the soccer team comes by, and she and Morgan start chatting about goalies. I stare at the floor, tracing imaginary patterns with my shoe. When I finally look back up I catch Blaine and Amber swaying back and forth to a slow song. I think back to the day I found him dancing around the guest room, belting out a Coldplay song. He's a lot more graceful and composed now; he isn't dancing awkwardly at all. In fact, he looks downright at ease with himself. As if being with Amber is the most comfortable, amazing feeling in the world.

"I'm going to get some fresh air," I mumble. I quickly make my way out of the gym and head toward the front of the school. Once I'm alone, I crouch down, placing my head in my hands.

I don't know how long I'm out there—five minutes, maybe—when I hear Morgan approach.

"I'm sorry you're so bummed, Nichols," she says, leaning back against the outside of the building. "Guys suck sometimes."

I snort. "You're telling me."

"It's depressing in there. Every way you look there are couples kissing, holding hands, laughing, talking. At least Amber and Gordon aren't making out. I haven't even seen him hold her hand."

"True," I admit, standing back up. "But it's going to be murder coming back to school on Monday. Everybody's going to be gossiping about how close they got at the big dance. I mean, it hurts no matter what. But it wouldn't be so bad if everyone weren't talking about it."

"No lie, this whole school is obsessed

with Gordon and Amber," Morgan says, running her fingers through her hair. "Even teachers are gossiping about it!"

I scrunch up my face in confusion. "Really? Like who."

"Well, Mr. Dimitri for one. He was way interested in Gordon."

Alarm bells go off in my head. "What do you mean 'way interested'?"

Morgan shrugs her shoulders. "He kept asking all these questions about Amber and Gordon. Mostly Gordon."

"What kind of stuff was he asking?" I'm starting to get really anxious.

"You know, how long he'd been going to school here. Where he's from. Normal stuff."

I fight hard to keep my voice steady. "Morgan, does Mr. Dimitri teach junior English?"

"No, just sophomore." She eyes me quizzically. "Why?"

"Because if he doesn't teach junior English, then how does he even know who Gordon is?"

She scratches her head. "Yeah, that's a good point. I hadn't thought of that."

My dad's warning runs through my

mind. *If anyone takes an unnatural interest in Blaine, let me know ASAP.* And then I remember it, and my body freezes. The day I tried to interview him about the new faculty plumbing, he slammed the door in my face and said, "I know you want to be a hotshot journalist like your mother." How did he know my mom is a journalist? I've never mentioned it. Not during homeroom and not during English class. Unless . . .

"Oh, shit!" I say, before I can stop myself.

"What's wrong, Nichols? You've gone all Casper on me."

"Morgan, do you know where Gordon is?" I ask, standing up. My knees are knocking together. "Was he still in the gym when you came out here?" I have to find Blaine and warn him. He's got to get out of here as soon as possible.

Morgan shakes her head. "Gordon disappeared off the dance floor a while ago. I think he and Amber might have snuck off to get some privacy. I'm sorry." She gives me a sympathetic smile.

Oh my God! "I have to go," I say, rushing around the front of the school. "I have to get in touch with my dad *now*!"

Morgan looks confused. "But your dad's going to be back in a few hours to pick us up," she points out. "Can't it wait until then?"

"No, it can't! It's extremely important that I talk to him right now!"

I can't get reception on my cell phone in front of the building, so we hurry outside to the back parking lot. Once we get to the edge of the faculty parking lot my reception kicks in and I start frantically dialing every number I have for Dad. He doesn't answer any of them, so I leave urgent messages telling him about Mr. Dimitri. Why the hell aren't they home? I try my mom's cell, but it goes straight to voice mail. Damn it! She never leaves the thing on when you need it.

"What am I going to do?" I wail. "This is horrible!"

Morgan places a hand on my shoulder. "Tell me what's going on. Maybe I can help."

I fight back waves of panic. "Blaine's in danger! Really serious, *gravely* serious, danger!"

"So his name *is* Blaine!" she says. "I knew it." The rest of the sentence registers with her. "No! You're not being serious, are you?"

I quickly fill Morgan in. At this point, it doesn't matter if she knows the truth. It's pretty obvious Blaine's cover has been compromised. Morgan's eyes grow larger and larger as I talk and, by the end of the story, they're about to pop out of their sockets.

She stands there for a minute, completely dazed, and then says, "Okay, we've gotta find him *now*. He's probably back in the locker rooms or something. You go track him down and I'll keep trying to call your dad," she says, whipping out her cell phone. "Everything's going to be okay," Morgan assures me. "You'll see. Mr. Dimitri might not even be who you think he is. Maybe it's just all a coincidence. And even if your worst fears are true . . . well, that doesn't mean he's planning on doing anything tonight. He's had his eye on Blaine for days now, and he hasn't done anything. There's no reason to think tonight is the night he's going to pounce. And this is all assuming Dimitri actually *is* up to something rotten. We don't know that yet."

"Thanks, Morgan." I'm starting to feel a little bit better. And then it happens. I spot something that makes my blood go cold. Parked at the far end of the faculty lot, underneath a big oak tree, is a dark blue Toyota Camry with a dent in the driver's-side door. Exactly like the one that nearly followed us home from The Cheesecake Factory that night.

"Morgan," I say, my voice shaking. "Whose car is that?"

Morgan gets to school really early and sees most of the teachers arriving. She knows what practically everyone drives. "Where?"

"Over there." I point. "The blue Toyota."

"That's Mr. Dimitri's ride." She looks alarmed. "That's not a bad sign or anything, is it?"

I don't answer her. I run into the school building at top speed, dashing through the corridors and into the gym. I frantically scan the room for Blaine. I catch sight of him by the bleachers, talking to Amber and a couple of upperclassmen. I breathe a huge sigh of relief. *He's okay!*

I've just started across the floor for him when I see Mr. Dimitri coming from the opposite direction. He's talking on a cell phone, and he's moving quickly. I pick up the pace, but it's tough getting through the crowd. I weave my way through the couples on the dance floor. I reach the other side of the gym just in time to see Mr. Dimitri leading Blaine out into the hallway. He's gripping Blaine tightly by the arm.

No! This can't be happening! My heart is racing at a million beats per second. I race after them, managing to slide through the double doors before they slam shut. Mr. Dimitri has no idea I'm behind them. He's practically dragging Blaine along now.

I'm incredibly scared, but I know it's up to me to stop them. And so, doing my best impression of Matt Damon in *The Bourne Identity*, I haul off and attempt to tackle Mr. Dimitri. I'm running at top speed when my ankle twists and I go tumbling forward. No Sydney Bristow, indeed. But I slam into Dimitri with such force that he topples to the ground and the cell phone goes flying.

I jump up quickly, brushing myself off. Blaine rushes to help me, but I push him back. "Get out of here!" I hiss. "Get as far away as you can."

"I'm not leaving you," Blaine says, looking shaken.

"You shouldn't have done that, kid,"

Mr. Dimitri snarls, standing up and reaching into his pocket for something.

I feel myself growing faint. It's a gun. I know it. He's got a gun. Before I can move a muscle I hear someone shout, "Don't even think about it!"

I whirl around. "Dad!"

I don't know where he's come from. Morgan must have gotten in touch with him. Dad has his gun drawn and aimed at Mr. Dimitri's head. "Don't move an inch. You hear me?"

The next few minutes happen so fast, I can barely process them. I stare in shock as my father throws Mr. Dimitri up against the wall and handcuffs him. I am speechless as a crowd of students gathers in the hall to watch as two uniformed police officers come rushing in and secure Mr. Dimitri, stripping him of his weapon and leading him out the door.

"Kaitlyn," Blaine says, putting his arm around my shoulders. "Are you all right?"

"I think so," I mumble.

"Thank God!" He puts his other arm around me and squeezes me tight. "That was horrible! I thought Mr. Dimitri was going to hurt you."

I feel faint, disoriented, as the reality of what just happened sinks in.

"You look so weak," Blaine says, placing one hand tenderly on my cheek. "Do you want to sit down?"

Before I can answer, everything goes black.

Twenty-one

"Where am I?" I ask, blinking furiously and looking around. I'm lying in a strange bed in a strange room. The walls are pale yellow and I hear something beeping behind me.

"Kaitlyn. You're awake!" It's my mother's voice.

"Mom," I say. "What's going on?"

"You're in the hospital."

The hospital? It all comes rushing back to me. The Valentine's Day dance. The blue Toyota Camry. Everything fading to black.

"How's Morgan?" I ask frantically. "Where is she?"

"She's fine," Mom says. "A little shaken up. But otherwise okay. She's planning to come see you tomorrow afternoon."

"How're you feeling, Kait?" Dad asks, coming into the room.

"Dad! Thank God you're here!" I shriek. I rush to get the story out all at once. "Mr.DimitriwastryingtokillBlaine."

"What?"

"MR. DIMITRI WAS TRYING TO KILL BLAINE!"

"I know," Dad says. "When I dropped you off at the dance I noticed the Toyota out in the parking lot. I started doing a little digging around and, before long, I figured out what was going on. I was in the process of calling for reinforcement when Morgan got in touch with me. I knew I couldn't wait, so I went in."

"But Blaine's okay, isn't he?" I ask.

"Blaine's safe. He's at the FBI office downtown. He'll be heading back to Texas later tonight."

"I have to see him." I struggle to get out of bed, but Dad stops me.

"Take it easy, Kaitlyn," he cautions. "The doctors don't want you up walking around just yet. You hit the ground pretty hard when you fainted."

"I fainted?" I ask, puzzled. That's a very unspylike thing to do. I can't remember any episodes of *Alias* where Sydney fainted.

"Yes, you did. You went out cold right as they were hauling off Lyle Gomar."

"Who?"

"You know him as Mr. Dimitri, but his real name is Lyle Gomar," Dad explains. "He's a notorious gun for hire. But don't worry. Thanks to your handiwork, we caught him. He was just about to grab Blaine when you tackled him with that pseudo karate move. Not that I'd recommend trying something similar again—you could have gotten seriously hurt—but it actually worked. You slowed Gomar down until I got there."

I struggle to understand. "This is crazy."

Dad fills me in on what went down. It turns out Lyle Gomar was hired to track down Blaine and his mother. Despite the FBI's best efforts, he managed to trace Blaine to St. Louis. But he still needed to find Mrs. Donovan, so that's why he hadn't made a move yet. He wanted to follow us for a while to see if we'd lead him to her.

"Gomar broke into Regina Kimble's house a couple of weeks ago and has been using it as a staging point. That's how he got her car. He's kept Mrs. Kimble tied up since then. He was there the night my colleague called to ask her about the car. Gomar was holding a gun to Mrs. Kimble's head, which is why she lied."

I gasp. "He had a gun to her head! Oh my gosh, is she okay?"

"She's pretty frail and upset, but she's doing okay. She's a little bit dehydrated, but Gomar didn't seriously harm her."

"What about Mr. Clemmons? Did this Lyle Gomar guy," I gulp, "do anything terrible to him?"

"No, that was just good luck on Gomar's part. He was angling to get a substitute teaching job at Copperfield when Mr. Clemmons's appendix ruptured."

"I never thought I'd say this, but I'm actually looking forward to seeing Mr. Clemmons again!" I say with relief.

My parents laugh. "I thought you might be," Dad says. "And you'll be happy to know that, when pressed, Lyle Gomar spilled everything about his employers. We've apprehended the people who were after Blaine's family. He's safe now."

I'm really happy for him, but it's kind of bittersweet. I was terrified earlier when I thought Blaine was in danger. Now I just miss him.

"There's something else," Dad says, taking my hand and squeezing it. "I owe you an apology. Both of you. I never should have put you in this position. When they asked me to do this job, I almost turned it down, and now I wish I had. I just felt so bad for that poor boy. And I thought that if my family was in that situation I'd want someone to help out. But, in hindsight, I never should have brought Blaine into our home. I had no idea things would reach this level, that a hit man would trace Blaine to St. Louis. I endangered the lives of my family. And I'll never forgive myself for that."

"No way!" I object. "You did the right thing."

Mom nods. "Blaine's heading back home now, safe and sound. The guys who were threatening his father have been apprehended."

"Wow, I can't believe Blaine's going back to Texas," I say, feeling a little sad. "I didn't even get to tell him good-bye."

"I'm sorry, honey," Mom says, patting me on the leg. "I know he understood."

"All in all, I'd say this job was an overwhelming success." Dad puts his arm around me. "I owe a lot of that to you, Kaitlyn. You were amazing." He smiles. "Who knows, you might have a career as a secret agent yet!"

I glance down at my hospital gown and bed. "I think I'll stick to journalism for now."

Mom grins. "Either way, you'll be following in one of our footsteps." She looks really proud.

"I'm sorry I fainted." I feel pretty silly. What kind of person faints because they're scared? Certainly not an elite spy.

"Why are you sorry?" Dad asks, looking confused.

"Because it's goofy. I totally overreacted. I mean, did you guys even hear the insane voice mails I left on your work phones? I was way panicked."

They exchange a glance. "Kaitlyn," Mom says, "that reminds me. There's something I need to tell you. I actually just got the news today, but with all the excitement I've been forgetting to tell you."

I eye her curiously. "Okay, give it to me."

"I know this isn't the best time, but we've kept this from you for long enough," Dad says.

"Well, don't keep me in suspense," I prod. "Tell me."

"I've suspected this for a while now, but the doctor confirmed it earlier," Mom says, grinning from ear to ear. "I'm pregnant."

My jaw drops. So I was right all along! I just lie there staring at them for a long time.

"Are you okay?" Mom asks. "We were worried about how you'd take it."

"I'm fine. Although it's a good thing I was already in a hospital bed when you told me," I joke. "Otherwise I might have fainted all over again."

Twenty-two

"I can't believe your cousin is a billionaire," Scott Ryder says, looking annoyed. "Nothing about that guy screamed money."

It's the following week and we're standing in the *Copperfield Courier* offices waiting for the staff meeting to begin. The entire school has been buzzing about Blaine's story ever since the dance. Miller even tried to strong-arm me into writing a first-person account of it. I politely declined. I field at least fifty questions a day about Blaine from other students. No need to invite more.

"So, Kaitlyn," Scott says as Miller calls the meeting to order. "I don't have a date for the Spring Fling next month. I thought you might want to go. Since you stupidly gave up the chance to go to the Valentine's dance with me."

I blink in surprise. "You mean you aren't asking Amber?"

"Nah," he says, smiling. "I tried. But she's boycotting all dances on principle. After what happened with Gordon and the psycho substitute teacher, she says she's completely over dances."

Just when I think Scott can't suck any worse, he goes and surprises me. "As tempting as it is to be sloppy seconds, I'll have to pass."

"Whatever." Scott shrugs. "Suit yourself," he says, and I think the issue is dropped. But after the meeting ends, he brings it up again. "Just so you know, Kaitlyn, I didn't really want to take *you*, anyway," he sneers. "I was merely trying to be nice. Save you from nerdville. But now I see that's hopeless. You're as bad as Morgan 'Geek Stink Breath' Riddick."

Did he just call her Geek Stink Breath? "How did you know about that?" I ask suspiciously. "I thought Amber wrote that on the chalkboard."

"It was my idea." Scott taps his iPod for emphasis. "Amber wanted an original insult and, since I'm a writer, I couldn't help giving her something good."

Why does this not surprise me? I'm all poised to fire off a round of insults but then I stop myself. He's not worth it. I'm running late, anyway. I've got to meet Morgan so we can head over to Union Station for a little shopping and Quiznos. It feels good that things are getting back to normal. The last thing I need is to butt heads with Scott Ryder.

"See you later, Scott," I say simply.

"Tell Gordon I said 'hi,'" Scott says, waving good-bye.

"Blaine," I correct him. "His name is Blaine."

"I wanted to show you something," Mom says later that night. She reaches into her bag and pulls out a folded-up piece of paper. "It's this week's column. It comes out tomorrow, but here's a sneak preview. I thought you should read it before it pubs."

The headline jumps out at me straight away: TEEN LOVE GROWS UP. Wh-what? I read the first paragraph: *Sometimes we don't give teenagers the credit they deserve. We're so quick to dismiss their romantic feelings as 'puppy love.' We don't take their relationships seriously. But maybe we should. Here's why.*

I scan the rest of the article in shock.

Mom's talking about me! And Blaine, of course. "Mom, what is this?" I ask.

"I hope you don't mind. I didn't use your name. Or any identifying details," she explains. "But I wanted to tell your and Blaine's story. It was a nice counterpoint to the piece I wrote a few weeks ago, about teen sex. I think so many parents—me included—jump the gun and panic when our teenagers start dating. We automatically assume that if a girl has a boyfriend, it means she's having sex. We think once hormones kick in good judgment flies out the window."

Oh my God, we're back on this cringe-worthy topic? I thought we left it behind weeks ago!

"But after watching you with Blaine, I realize how wrong that is," Mom continues.

"You do?" I ask, my eyes growing wide.

Mom smiles. "It was so sweet watching you and Blaine together. The way you were star-crossed, but then you accepted fate. You accepted when it wasn't in the cards for you to have a relationship, and you let him go. People always think of teens as being so irrational when they're in love. I wanted to tell the other side of the story."

I blush. "Thanks. I think."

"Also, it was good to have a break from writing about crotchless panties," Mom says, rolling her eyes.

"Ew!" I shriek. "That was one phrase I never needed to hear you say."

"Sorry," Mom apologizes. "So, are you excited about the baby?"

I smile. "Yeah, I am." This is the truth. I've always wanted a brother or sister. Being an only child gets lonely sometimes. "You know, I sort of figured out you were pregnant a while back."

Mom clutches her stomach playfully. "Don't tell me I was already showing a few weeks ago!"

"No, no. But when you started talking about going to see Dr. Gifford and about the house becoming more crowded, I kind of put two and two together."

Mom's thoughtful. "When was that?"

"The night Blaine got here, actually. I kept meaning to ask you about it but there was so much excitement with him being here. And I also kinda figured you'd tell me when you were ready."

"You really are growing up." She studies my face for a minute. "You miss him, don't you?"

"Yeah," I admit sheepishly. "I guess that kind of goes against the point of your column."

"Not at all. Missing him is normal. Now, if you'd hopped on a Greyhound bus to Texas, then *that* would be going against the column."

I giggle despite myself. "I just wish I could talk to Blaine," I say. "It ended on such weird terms between us. I didn't even get to say good-bye. And now I can't contact him. I don't even have his e-mail address."

"Maybe you can," Mom says, grinning. "I bet if you gave Dad a letter, he could pass it on to Blaine."

"Really?" I ask.

"I don't see why it would be a problem."

"Thanks, Mom!" I give her a hug. Then I go upstairs to get cracking. It takes me over an hour to compose a letter even though, in the end, it's only one page long.

Dear Blaine,
I hope you don't mind me writing you like this. You left so abruptly and there are a lot of things I want to say. It's strange not being able to walk down the hall when I want to talk to

you. But I'm happy that everything worked out and you got to go back home safely.

I'd be lying if I said I didn't miss you. I'd also be lying if I said I didn't like you. You know, in THAT way. I feel embarrassed writing this down on paper, but it's the truth. I like you. I've liked you from the moment I met you. Even as I was trying to karate chop you to oblivion, I was secretly thinking, "Wow, this guy is amazing." And the more I got to know you, the more amazing you became. You're so smart, caring, funny and, of course, cute. Okay, cute is probably not a strong enough word to describe you. But I think I'll stop there, 'cause I'm already blushing about fifty shades of red.

I wish things could have worked out differently between us. Call it a colossal case of bad timing. Or call it a twist of fate. I know I should accept that and move on, but, still, I keep wondering "What if?" That one kiss we shared was . . . unbelievable. I wish there could have been more.

To be totally honest, I've never felt

this way about anyone before. And it
will probably be a long time before I feel
this way again. I realize this doesn't
mean a lot right now. But I wanted you
to know.

> *Yours,*
> *Kaitlyn*

I'll probably never hear back from him,
but that's okay. This is something that I
have to do. I seal the letter in an envelope
and write Blaine's name on the front. I add
an a.k.a. Gordon Dennis Nichols in small
letters, just to be funny.

Then I track down Dad in the kitchen.
He's having a cup of coffee. My father is the
only person I know who drinks, like, a pot
of coffee at night. Never in the mornings,
always before bed. "Hey, Dad, I was wondering something . . ." I begin, turning the
envelope over in my hands.

"You want me to get a letter to Blaine?"

"Mom talked to you," I say.

He sets his coffee mug down on the
table. "Actually, no. I deduced it from the
writing on the front. You see that part there
where it's addressed to Blaine Donovan?" he
teases. "That's kind of a dead giveaway."

"Hardy har har." But I laugh despite myself.

"What did you write?" Dad asks, taking the letter from my hands.

"Uh, hello, nosy much?" I say.

He stirs his coffee. "It's personal, huh? Okay then. I'll just wait till I get to work to steam it open."

"Dad!"

"I'm only kidding," he says, giving me an exaggerated wink. "I don't need to steam it open. I work for the FBI, remember? We have better methods."

Twenty-three

It takes a few weeks for things to get back to normal at Cop-a-Feel High. At first, it feels like the Blaine Donovan story will never die down. But it eventually does. Amber continues to screw with people—she even spins the Blaine story to make it look like she rejected him. Scott moves on and starts dating Amber's friend Kayla.

As for me, I'm still dateless. I fill my time hanging out with Morgan and working on articles for the paper.

I'm sitting in my bedroom one night, reading over my history notes, when I hear a knock on the door.

"Come in," I mumble, not looking up.

"Hi," a guy's voice says.

No. It can't be. *Blaine!* I gasp, jumping up off the bed. "Oh my God! What are you doing here?" I ask, astonished.

"I came to see you."

"You *did*?" I don't know what to say to this. I can't believe he's here, standing right in front of me. I actually pinch myself to make sure it's real.

He grins. "I got your letter." He reaches into his jeans pocket and pulls it out. It's all crumpled up, like he's read it a million times. "This meant a lot to me," he says softly. "I've been wanting to see you ever since I read it."

I grab hold of my desk chair to steady myself. I'm so shocked to see him. "How did you get here?"

"My father wanted to come to St. Louis on business. I begged him to let me tag along."

I swing the door to my bedroom open wide and invite him in. "It's great to see you."

"It's great to see you, too." We stand there looking at each other for a long moment.

"Kaitlyn—," he begins.

"Blaine—," I say simultaneously.

We both laugh. "You first," he says.

"I forgot what I was going to say," I giggle.

"Me, too." Blaine leans forward and kisses me. It's awesome and intense, and every bit as good as the kiss we had that day in the newsroom. Better, even.

"Who needs words?" I say, when we pull apart.

He leans forward and rests his forehead against mine. "I missed you," he says, his breath tickling my face.

"I missed you, too."

He moves back until he's looking in my eyes. "I meant what I told you. I do like you. And I *do* want to go out with you. If you're willing to give it a try."

It feels great to hear him say that. But I worry. "How can it work?" I ask. "Texas and St. Louis aren't exactly close by. And long-distance relationships never work."

"They don't?" he asks. "Have you ever had one?"

"Uh, not exactly. But I hear things."

Blaine kisses me again, briefly this time. "I'll be going to college in just over a year. Who knows? Maybe I could find a school nearby. Or you could go to school in Texas. Until then, I'm up for a long-distance relationship if you are."

He is? I'm dizzy with excitement at the thought of being with him. "I want to. I just worry it will be so hard to make it work."

"We can talk on the phone every day, visit each other on the weekends."

I wrap my arms tightly around his waist. "Visit? But Texas is so far away."

"Hey, I have a private plane, remember?" Blaine takes my hand in his.

"I want this," I tell him, squeezing his hand in mine. "I want to be with you."

"Then you will be." He kisses me again, then pulls apart. "Just do one thing for me?"

"Sure, anything." I lean against him, savoring the moment.

"Never, *ever* call me Gordon again."

"Deal." We shake on it.

"Oh, and one more thing."

I nod.

"No more secrets. No more lying, hiding, keeping all of this undercover. Let's be out in the open from now on. Okay?"

"My thoughts exactly," I say, smiling.

In a way I suppose I'll miss my life as a junior secret agent. It definitely had some exciting moments. But overall, I'm happy to get back to being plain, average, boring Kaitlyn Nichols.

Although with Blaine by my side, I can't imagine things will ever be boring again.

About the Author

Jo Edwards is the bestselling author of two adult novels. She is an award-winning journalist who has written for *Woman's Day* and *Figure* magazines. She lives in Memphis, Tennessee, where she spends her days stalking Justin Timberlake and working on her next book.

LOL at this sneak peek of

Prom Crashers
By Erin Downing

A new Romantic Comedy from Simon Pulse

☆

"Speaking of prom—again," Emily said, attempting to head off another bickering session between Charlie and Sid. "I have a date."

Max, Sid, and Charlie turned. The looks on their faces suggested disbelief.

"What?" she said, giving them each a look. "You don't believe me?"

"We're constantly with you," Charlie said in response. "When would you have had time to get yourself a date that we wouldn't know about?"

"Let me clarify. I have a date if I can *find* him again."

"You do or you don't have a date?" Max looked confused and a little ill. The grapefruit seemed to be messing with him.

"I met the guy last night at the mall. His name is Ethan."

"Cut!" Charlie yelled, clinking the ice

cubes in his empty lemonade glass over his head like a maraca. "I was *there*, remember? You don't even have his number, if I'm not mistaken. My apologies for that."

Charlie had already apologized a million times for his goof the night before. After Emily had run out the mall doors after Ethan and searched the parking lot until she was sure he was nowhere to be found, she and Charlie couldn't help but laugh a little. Fate played funny games. . . . She was clearly destined not to go to prom. But she wasn't willing to give up that easily.

Emily lifted her hand. "Clarification. I *had* his number. But you're correct—I no longer have his number. Which means we have some plotting to do."

"Is this another Emily plan?" Max asked, leaning his head back into the grass. He waved his fingers in the air and chanted, "Go, Tigers! Yay!" He was clearly thinking about Emily's sophomore year plot to try out for the cheerleading squad, even though she hated cheerleading. She just thought it would be funny. "Because honestly, your plans sort of scare me." Like he was one to talk.

"Ding ding ding!" Emily replied, clapping. "I have a plan."

She continued, "Here's what I know about this guy. One, he is going to prom because he was shopping for his tux. And P.S., he's going with his sister's friend, not a girlfriend, and he was definitely flirting with me—so this isn't some delusional one-way street. Two, his name is Ethan. Three, he doesn't go to Humphrey." She paused, flicking a leaf that had floated over her foot in the wading pool. "So . . . we go where we know he will be! Let's find a way to get into all the *other* proms in the city and find this guy. It's *something* to do to kill the time, right?"

"Oh my God. We would be *Prom Crashers*!" Charlie looked thrilled.

"So does this mean you're in?" Emily asked hopefully.

Charlie nodded. "Absolutely."

Emily looked at the other two expectantly.

"What?" Sid asked. "You have Charlie. Why do you need me?"

Max grunted from his post on the ground. "What she said."

"You guys!" Emily stuck out her foot

and rolled Max onto his side on the grass so he was facing her. "We have to do this together. One last fling before we all take off for college. The ultimate challenge. What do you say?"

"I say," Sid said, chewing her Pop-Tart with her mouth open, "screw prom. I'm not going to my own—why would I want to go to someone else's?"

Charlie pushed his lip out in a pout. "I need you, Sid."

"Forget it," Emily retorted. "I'm not begging. But it's going to be a blast. That's all I'm saying. I know *I* need something to get me through the rest of this year. I mean, this is the last month or whatever of our last year of high school. It would be fun to go out in style, the four of us, you know?" She blew her bangs out of her face and crossed her arms over her chest. "Whatever. You guys can spend the next month studying by yourselves. Charlie and I are going to kick some butt crashing proms. Harrumph." She had a faint smile tugging at the corners of her mouth.

Sid shrugged and glanced at Max. "Fine. I'm in." She grinned meekly. "When you put it that way."

"Nuh-uh," Emily shook her finger. "Not like that. If you're in, you're in. No half-hearted 'fine.'" She made quotes in the air.

Charlie snickered. "Tough guy. I like it."

"I'm in! I'm in!" Sid sarcastically cheered her arms in the air. "Better? I'll take anything to kill the time until we graduate. It sounds sort of fun." She shrugged. "Besides, you literally couldn't drag me to my own prom. So this is a good way to see what this prom crap is all about. Do I get to wear pink?"

"I'll do it on one condition," Max broke in, pushing himself up on his elbows on the ground. He was laughing at the image of Sid in pink.

"Yes?" Emily prompted. She was giddy with the hope that this might actually happen. She could think of no better way to celebrate prom season—and get a date— than with a crazy challenge.

Max looked at Emily sternly. "This is about the quest. I couldn't care less about finding this guy—it just sounds like a good time. You promise you won't get all serious and psycho-stalker?"

"Come on . . . you know me. Who would be more into the adventure than me?

This is totally about the quest." She looked innocent, and laughed when Max continued to look at her sharply.

"Fine," he agreed. "But promise anyway. This is *not* just about the guy."

She nodded seriously. "I promise. Of course, I *want* to find Ethan. But prom crashing is the perfect distraction to kill the time before we get out of this lame town. And if we succeed in our mission, I will have a superfoxy date. What could be better than that?"

"We have nine targets." Charlie had spread paper beverage napkins across the counter at the Leaf Lounge. Each napkin had the name of one of the area high schools written on it. He and Emily were working the Wednesday night shift, and Charlie had spent most of it plotting their first move for Operation: Prom Crashing.

Max, who was sitting on Frank's stool at the counter, had come to the mall partly to plan, partly to flesh out his latest story pitch (a feature about some local guy who carved bears out of cheese rind), and partly to catch the tail end of Sid's set.

Sid often played her guitar and sang in

the evenings at the Leaf Lounge. Gary, the owner, thought she gave the place a cool vibe, and Sid was happy to have the venue. She was trying to get her start somewhere, and while she realized the mall coffee shop wasn't the Knitting Factory in New York, at least it gave her practice playing in front of a live crowd.

As was often the case, though, the "crowd" was only two people strong—Max, of course, and Vern, a cashier from Dylan's, the mall department store, who had hustled over to hear her play during his break. Vern always came to Sid's sets—he fashioned himself her biggest fan. He was maybe her *only* nonfriend fan. Sid's ultimate goal was to spend her life touring the country to play small clubs in big cities. But the first step was to extend her reach beyond the mall's walls and gain a slightly cooler fan base.

Her bluesy-rock sound was fabulous. She just needed her break.

As Sid struck the final chord of her last song, Vern broke into mad applause. Emily rolled her eyes. Sid dropped her guitar into its case and strolled over to the counter, with a brief nod in Vern's direction.

"Complimentary beverage?" Emily asked. "Great set."

"Coffee?" Sid grabbed one of the napkins off the counter and studied it. She didn't like to talk about her performances—she always said that the lack of audience was painfully depressing. "What's all this?"

"All this," Charlie explained, "is the beginning of a plan. Did everyone do their homework this week?"

The other three nodded. After agreeing to Emily's prom-crashing plan the previous weekend, each of them had contacted everyone they knew, trying to get intelligence about all the other proms around the city so they could formulate a plan. As they reported their findings, Charlie pulled out each school's napkin and scribbled out the date and location of its prom.

Emily studied the napkins and began to sort them into piles. "We have four weekends. Nine proms."

"We can count out our own schools," Max said, plucking the napkins with South and Humphrey written on them. "We know Ethan won't be there, right? Charlie, Sid, you checked South's directory for an

Ethan?" Charlie nodded. "So that's only seven. Not bad."

Sid slapped her hand on the counter. "Totally doable."

"We have a big weekend ahead of us," Emily said, grinning. "Three this Saturday—Marshall, Park, and Memorial."

"Like, three days from now?" Max asked, sounding mildly concerned.

"Yup. You worried?" Emily poked him in the arm. He poked her back. Emily hoped he was eating real food again, and not just grapefruit. Otherwise, he'd be really crabby for their first proms.

Charlie shuffled three of the napkins so they were lined up in front of him on the counter. "All right," he said, suddenly very businesslike. "What's our strategy for these first three? Do we just break in? Show up? How are we gonna do this?"

Emily chewed her lower lip thoughtfully. "Well, I guess we could just sneak in," she said finally. "Though that seems a little boring."

"And not possible at Memorial," Sid said, sipping her coffee. "The guy I know who goes there said security is really tight on the day of prom. The dance itself is held in Memorial's gym. They lock all the doors a few hours before prom starts to keep the unsavory types out. And it's a superstrict ticket system. I guess the parents all get a little paranoid for their precious babies' security."

"Okay." Emily nodded. "So sneaking in isn't an option at Memorial. Maybe we could plant someone on the inside before they lock the doors?"

Charlie clapped. "I like that!"

"The other two are both at the convention center," Max broke in. He had found the details about Marshall's and Park's proms online. "So maybe we divide and conquer? Two of us go to Marshall and Park, the other two to Memorial?"

"Yeah," Emily said, "that would be good, except I'm the only one who knows what Ethan looks like. The point of our mission, remember?"

Max rolled his eyes. "Ah, yes . . . the guy."

"Ethan," Emily corrected. "Plus, isn't this more fun if we all do it together? Max, what if you and I try to break in to Marshall and Park, then meet up with Sid and Charlie at Memorial later? They could sneak into the school that afternoon and hang out, then let us in through an unguarded door when we get there?"

"Nice." Charlie waved the napkin with Memorial written on it. "My first conquest."

Sid raised her hand. "One other tiny issue," she said, waiting to get their attention. "I have nothing to wear."

"I can borrow my dad's tux," Max declared proudly. "It might be a little big and boxy, but it's free. If I'm not going to my own prom, I'm not paying to rent one." Max didn't have a date for prom. He and Emily had sort of joked about going together as "worst-case scenario" dates, but neither had actually bought tickets. So it didn't look like it was going to happen.

"I own a tux, so I'm good," Charlie said. "I feel a little weird wearing the same shirt more than once, but I guess since it will be different crowds at each prom, I can break the rule."

Emily and Sid exchanged a look. "Since I'm not *officially* going to prom—yet—it might be a little tough to convince my parents to buy me a dress. I'd have to do too much explaining. How about you, Sid?"

"Nothing. And I'm not borrowing from my mom. Nuh-uh. No way. She wears shoulder pads."

"So we can either buy something or go with what we have. We'll obviously look out of place in jeans, which makes crashing a little more challenging."

Sid nodded. "I'm going to propose a third option, since I refuse to buy a dress." She jumped off her stool. "Max, can you cover for Em? Charlie doesn't do anything, and someone has to serve the customers while I steal Emily for two secs."

"Hey!" Charlie feigned anger but knew he had no right to be defensive.

"I don't even know what a macchiato is," Max responded. "But yeah, I can cover." He moved behind the counter as Emily slid past him and untied her apron.

"What's the plan?" she asked as Sid pulled her into the mall.

"You're about to see me do something *very* scary. If you laugh, I'll bite. I mean it."